IN TOO DEEP

IN TOO DEEP

an ELITE novel

jennifer banash

BERKLEY JAM, NEW YORK

THE BERKLEY PUBLISHING GROUP
Published by the Penguin Group
Penguin Group (USA) Inc.
375 Hudson Street, New York, New York 10014, USA

Penguin Group (Canada), 90 Eglinton Avenue East, Suite 700, Toronto, Ontario M4P 2Y3, Canada
(a division of Pearson Penguin Canada Inc.)
Penguin Books Ltd., 80 Strand, London WC2R 0RL, England
Penguin Group Ireland, 25 St. Stephen's Green, Dublin 2, Ireland (a division of Penguin Books Ltd.)
Penguin Group (Australia), 250 Camberwell Road, Camberwell, Victoria 3124, Australia
(a division of Pearson Australia Group Pty. Ltd.)
Penguin Books India Pvt. Ltd., 11 Community Centre, Panchsheel Park, New Delhi—110 017, India
Penguin Group (NZ), 67 Apollo Drive, Rosedale, North Shore 0632, New Zealand
(a division of Pearson New Zealand Ltd.)
Penguin Books (South Africa) (Pty.) Ltd., 24 Sturdee Avenue, Rosebank, Johannesburg 2196,
South Africa

Penguin Books Ltd., Registered Offices: 80 Strand, London WC2R 0RL, England

This book is an original publication of The Berkley Publishing Group.

This is a work of fiction. Names, characters, places, and incidents either are the product of the author's imagination or are used fictitiously, and any resemblance to actual persons, living or dead, business establishments, events, or locales is entirely coincidental. The publisher does not have any control over and does not assume any responsibility for author or third-party websites or their content.

PRINTING HISTORY
Berkley JAM trade paperback edition / January 2009

Library of Congress Cataloging-in-Publication Data

Banash, Jennifer.
In too deep / Jennifer Banash. — Berkley JAM trade paperback ed.
    p. cm.
"An Elite Novel."
Summary: While Madison ponders revenge and a possible modeling career, Casey fears she has lost herself by adapting fully to luxurious New York City life, and Phoebe keeps a secret, Sophie seeks to bring her birth mother to her sixteenth-birthday party.
ISBN 978-0-425-22353-6
[1. Interpersonal relations—Fiction. 2. Wealth—Fiction. 3. Mothers and daughters—Fiction.
4. Identity—Fiction. 5. Dating (Social customs)—Fiction. 6. New York (N.Y.)—Fiction.]
I. Title.
PZ7.B2176In 2009
[Fic]—dc22

                                                                                              2008039858

147204767

acknowledgments

I'd like to thank Kate Seaver, my wonderful editor at Berkley, who took a chance on an unknown kid; my agent, Jennifer Jackson, who always has my back; and Willy Blackmore, who read every draft and kept me sane through the entire process. To all the YA bloggers and teen reviewers everywhere—thanks for getting the word out and making my books matter—I am eternally grateful. And, most of all, I'd like to give a huge shout-out to all the readers of The Elite series—you are the reason I sit in front of a computer for hours at a time, dreaming up what comes next.

Who's your best friend? Who's your worst enemy?

"One can never really know . . . Enemy? Who cares?"
—KARL LAGERFELD,
Elle MAGAZINE, SEPTEMBER 2007

hot lunch

Madison Macallister straightened the silken sleeve of her floral-patterned black and crimson wrap dress, and stabbed her fork into the desiccated remains of her smoked salmon salad, bringing a mouthful of baby greens up to her matte ruby-red lips. If she kept on eating this way, she was definitely going to blow up—and not in a good way. She was already changing into her baggy sweats the second she got home from school every day, and the waistband of her favorite new Citizens of Humanity jeans was decidedly snugger than when she bought them in a depression-fueled shopping incident a few weeks ago—a binge of Posh and Becks–worthy proportions that resulted in Edie storming into her room and cutting up her Amex Black card right in front of her. Madison exhaled deeply, spearing the last hunk of salty smoked fish and popping it into her mouth while checking out the six-carat square-cut emerald ring that shone brilliantly on her ring finger, winking in the fluorescent lighting. It had been worth it.

Besides, now that she was more miserable than ever, it seemed crucial to have a few things in her life that actually gave her pleasure—and shopping was definitely one of them. Drew may have been history, but at least she had her new black leather Furla tote trimmed in the softest gray fox fur *ever* to console her. Madison was beginning to see that boyfriends came and went with alarming speed, and friends were clearly not to be trusted. But clothes? Clothes never let you down. And accessories were forever . . .

It had been three weeks since Drew's party—three long, agonizing weeks as the leaves in Central Park began turning orange, then red; the nights growing progressively cooler. More often than not, Madison found herself reaching for a sweater to throw over her shoulders in the early mornings, and pulling her caramel-colored Hermès riding gloves over cold hands that felt more like icicles than fingers. And even though the weather was definitely changing, things between her and Drew were not. Much like the first chilly days of winter—which were definitely now on the way—their relationship had completely frosted over. When they passed each other in the hall, Drew dipped his eyes away from her gaze and stared at the floor—especially if he happened to be walking with Casey. It had gone on for so long now that even if for some bizarre reason they did end up talking again she wouldn't have the faintest idea what to *say*. Somehow—at least for her anyway—it was easier this way. Out of sight, out of mind—just like her credit card bills.

And if she wasn't thinking about the way he'd clearly dumped her for Casey, she didn't have to deal with the fact that he might just prefer someone else to her. But, no matter how hard she tried, Madison just couldn't wrap her head around the idea. How was that even *possible*? And the only thing that even remotely put a crimp in her plans to pretend they'd both been inexplicably eaten by dinosaurs was the fact that she had to see the both of them every fucking day at school. And, worse yet, Drew didn't even seem to care—it was as if their entire past had been wiped out with the arrival of one frizzy Midwestern freak with absolutely zero sex appeal, and who, despite her town of origin, was anything but "normal." Did the last two years mean nothing to him? Not only was this turn of events totally inconceivable, it was ruining her reputation! Everyone south of Park Avenue knew that Madison Macallister was the girl who got what she wanted—when she wanted it—and boys were no exception. Until now.

It was the start of junior year, and that being said, not only was it time for sweater shopping at TSE's annual fall sale, but it was also unfortunately the beginning of endless amounts of prep courses, practice exams, and untold amounts of worrying about the upcoming SATs. Not to mention the rapidly approaching nightmare of college applications once the exam was finally over, coupled with the enormous, looming question of what exactly she was going to do for the rest of her fucking life. Madison didn't waste her time pondering these kinds of questions—mostly because she didn't have the first clue how to answer them. Choosing just one thing to do for the rest of your life seemed so . . . limiting. And limits were for tiny people with tiny minds—not for card-carrying members of the over-privileged set, who were supposed to have options as wide as the Atlantic.

But when it came right down to it, Madison wasn't exactly sure *what* it was that she was really good at in the first place—with the possible exceptions of gossiping and accessorizing. So, at parties, when the topic turned, as it inevitably did, to the future, Madison had made it a habit recently of smiling prettily, and then changing the subject so fast that her audience was left with a bad case of social whiplash. It was unthinkable. Madison Macallister, otherwise known as Ms. Perfect of the Upper East Side, without a plan? Not only could it destroy her reputation as the ultimate Upper East Side robot princess, but it was also a potential embarrassment just waiting to happen. And Madison Macallister had made it a policy long ago to never, ever do embarrassing. If you were going to get all whiny and blubbery, you might as well just raise a white flag in the air, start wearing sweatpants to school, and just fucking surrender what was left of your dignity. The very idea of it made her shiver, her tiny, ski-slope nose wrinkling in distaste.

"*Look,*" Sophie whispered under her breath, diamond studs glinting in her honey hair, the majority of which was obscured by an Anna Kula gray knit cap. "Check out the happy couple—major bonding at twelve o'clock," she added in a conspiratorial, fake espionage voice. Ever since *The Bourne Ultimatum* came out on DVD Sophie wouldn't shut up about spies and the CIA. Not to mention Matt Damon's impressive biceps that fairly bulged beneath that hideously grungy jacket he wore for most of the movie.

And speaking of slightly crazier, fashion-obsessed wardrobes, in celebration of the rapidly approaching fall weather, Sophie was wearing a pair of gray wool, wide-leg pants and a white silk blouse with an enormous, loopy bow tied at the neck. An oversized leopard Jimmy Choo clutch sat on the table in front of her, and she absentmindedly stroked it while continuing to stare over Madison's head, her glossy pink lips parted. After years of being a veritable slave to Mystic Tan, Sophie had mysteriously halted her spray tan obsession immediately following Drew's party with no explanation whatsoever, and, as a result, her creamy skin glowed, her face rosy from just a hint of cherry-red cream blush rubbed onto the apples of her cheeks. Now that both Sophie and Phoebe were so scarily pale, Madison had taken to calling both of them the cadaver twins on account of the fact that they looked like they belonged in a fucking coffin.

As if she'd somehow read her mind, Phoebe raised her head from her iPhone and quit her incessant texting to glance across the room, her fingers halted on the keypad, her dark hair shining around her pale, heart-shaped face as she sang along with Jay-Z and Rihanna as they blared through the dining hall's sound system. *You can stand under my umbrella . . . ella . . . ella . . . eh.* Rihanna sounded as like she had been cursed with a truly unfortunate, incurable stutter—or a case of Tourette's. Madison rolled her green eyes, exhaling heavily. If she had to sit through this song one more time, she was going to stab herself in the eye with a fork. And if whatever spectacle going on behind her required actual *movement*, then it had better be good.

Madison stretched her arms over her head, and carefully turned around, her green cat eyes sweeping the crowded room, and settling uncomfortably on Casey and Drew, who were standing over at the coffee kiosk. Like they'd be anywhere else—Drew was so addicted to caffeine there should've been a twelve-step program founded in his honor. Casey was wearing a pair of faded jeans and a white sweater that looked like it came from some horrible suburban outlet store. Even so, Madison had to admit that as happy as Casey looked at that moment it wouldn't have mattered if she were wearing a paper bag. Casey's cheeks glowed pinkly and her irrepressibly curly hair waved down her back in yellow curls that shone in the glaring overhead light. She was still the total definition of a hot mess though—albeit a *happy* hot mess. Drew, of course, was yummy perfection as usual—even though his dark hair fell into his eyes, obscuring them from view. Clearly it was time for a haircut—and the loose, white button-down shirt he wore was splattered with coffee stains. Drew was nothing if not a total slob, but it didn't matter. He was still a vision in khakis. And as she watched Drew feed Casey a bit of a ginormous chocolate chunk cookie, Madison felt like she was about to claw her way out of her own decidedly green skin.

"They really are kind of ridiculously cute together in a Saturday-morning-cartoons-and-Lucky-Charms kind of way," Phoebe said after noticing Madison's unbroken gaze toward the coffee kiosk.

"Lucky Charms make me want to vomit. Seriously," Madison said. She was having none of this cutesy bullshit.

"You don't like Lucky Charms?" Sophie practically screamed.

"I LOVE Lucky Charms. I would always eat all the cereal bits first so the marshmallows would get all soft and the milk would turn purple . . ."

"ME TOO!" Phoebe squealed, interrupting her and then attacking her phone again as it beeped noisily.

"I'm not talking about cereal, damnit," Madison interrupted, trying to hold herself back from spitting her pent-up venom all over Sophie. "And who the hell are you texting anyway?" she snapped, pointing at Phoebe's phone. "We're practically your only friends." Phoebe's face turned crimson as she giggled nervously, shoving her phone into her oversized Tod's cream-colored leather tote that perfectly matched her ivory pants and cabled-cashmere sweater.

"Well, we're the most *important* anyway." Sophie giggled, leaning over and sipping her iced hazelnut latte through a red plastic straw. "Did I tell you guys that we finally found a location for my party?" Sophie asked. Her green eyes were bright with excitement as she pushed her latte away and began absentmindedly flipping though the pages of her cocoa-colored Hermès leather notebook she used to take notes in AP Algebra class, the pages filled with neat mathematical diagrams in precise purple ink. "And, oh my God, it's going to be soooo amazing! Just last night I heard that . . ."

Madison sighed in exasperation and turned away, staring off into space, the sounds of Sophie and Phoebe's incessant gossiping fading away like a bad radio signal. How could they not understand that what was going on in front of them was downright treasonous? In fact, it was an assault against all that the sovereign nation of Madison Macallister stood for. She had a mind to have Phoebe call Jason Bourne in to put a hit on the two for their crime against her. Or maybe there was another way . . .

Madison turned back to her empty plate and smiled as she pushed it away from her. She knew from experience that the best way to recapture a guy's interest was usually by getting interested in someone else, and Drew was definitely no exception. Besides, all guys were basically the same entity anyway—all they wanted was what they couldn't have. As soon as Drew saw her with another guy, he'd want her back all over again. She knew he'd start sending her flowers, showing up at her doorstep, basically groveling—and she was going to enjoy every ego-boosting minute of it.

Madison watched as Drew leaned in and gave Casey a long kiss good-bye, his hands on her shoulders, his fingers buried in her hair. Let him kiss whomever he wanted . . . now. By next week, she'd have a new boyfriend, and then he was going to be *really* sorry. Just the thought of her being interested in someone else would make him completely crazy—even if he didn't know it yet. And just because she got played didn't mean she had to sit around moping all year long, did it? Manhattan was a big city—and there were more than enough cute guys to distract her while she got this Drew problem ironed out. And, with Drew out of the picture, the Casey situation would naturally take care of itself: Before the fall term was over, her frizzy ass would be on a bus back to Nebraska, or wherever the hell she was from. *Count on it,* Madison thought as Casey tentatively approached the table, a bashful smile on her glowing, freckled face.

As much as it killed her to do so, Madison parted her lips

and smiled back, remembering the advice her mother, Edith Spencer Macallister, had given her after Becca McCormick had the nerve to declare on the first day of fifth grade—and in front of the entire class—that Madison Macallister was a stuck up little priss:

Keep your friends close and your enemies closer . . .

the
spanish
inquisition

Casey walked over to The Bram Clan's table, the imprint of Drew's lips still lingering on her mouth as Madison's icy green eyes regarded her with obvious disdain before quickly turning away. Casey watched with growing unease as Madison pulled a pair of huge Valentino shades over her eyes like a very expensive, couture smokescreen. Ever since Casey and Drew had become a "thing" (she still wasn't sure exactly what to call it, and asking him seemed like a decidedly bad idea), she'd gotten the feeling that, although she didn't seem angry, Mad was basically just tolerating her presence most of the time. And, as if that wasn't bad enough, the big question that Casey couldn't help turning over again and again in her mind was why wasn't Madison *more* pissed off? Not that she really *wanted* her to be or anything, but the fact that she was as cool as ever just didn't seem to make sense—unless she really *was* over it. Maybe she just really didn't care about Drew or want him for herself anymore . . .

Right, Casey thought, sitting down in an empty chair next to Sophie. *And monkeys will momentarily fly out of my butt.*

"Well, if it isn't Juliet," Phoebe chirped with a small smile while picking apart a fat-free blueberry muffin with her short, white-lacquered nails. Phoebe liked to absentmindedly obliterate whatever she happened to be eating—before it ever made the short journey from her fingers to her mouth. It came across as totally mindless, but Casey knew that it was actually something Phoebe forced herself to do on a daily basis so that she wouldn't scarf down the entire thing in two bites. Better to act like you didn't really care about food at all than to come off as a giant pig. "Where's Romeo running off to?" she asked as Drew paused at the door to the dining hall and turned, raising one hand in the air at Casey with a grin, before ducking through the door and out of sight.

"I think he's got AP Film . . . or maybe Chem," Casey mumbled, her face flooded with heat.

"Funny thing, chemistry . . ." Sophie added with a sly smile, stealing a hunk of Phoebe's crumbled muffin and popping it into her mouth as Madison glared at her disapprovingly from behind her shades. "I never did understand what Juliet saw in Romeo anyway—he's totally DNDL if you ask me."

"Good thing nobody's asking you," Madison said with a snort.

"What's DNDL?" Casey looked at Sophie quizzically. Why did it always seem like whenever it came to The Bram Clan there was a secret code she was never going to crack, even if she worked at it night and day?

"Date now, dump later," Phoebe said, splaying her fingers out and inspecting her manicure, which was predictably perfect. Did she do her nails every single night? Casey wondered, looking over at the smooth polish. She'd never seen Phoebe have so much as a chip. It just wasn't natural. Casey looked down at her own nails, which were ragged and bitten almost all the way down to her cuticles, and promptly hid them under the table.

"Not that you'd know anything about it," Madison said coolly, picking up her glass of Perrier with a bright green lime wedge the color of her eyes smashed at the bottom. "You don't really date—*or* dump." She sipped her fancy water, her lips set in a smirk.

"But I *will*," Phoebe said with impatience. "I'm just *choosy*."

"More like petrified," Madison answered as she retrieved a Lancôme lipstick from her Furla tote and ran the baby pink stain over her lips with a practiced hand. How the hell did she do that without using a mirror? Casey marveled while staring at Mad's perfect pout. Casey could barely apply ChapStick without getting it everywhere—much less anything that involved actual color and a steady hand . . . *Further proof that she's some kind of alien grown in a pod in outer space*, Casey thought as Mad threw her lipstick back into her tote, and pushed her platinum hair from her shoulders with a graceful swing of her head. *Kind of like Katie Holmes . . .*

"So, speaking of dating . . . how are things with the

Drewster?" Sophie turned to Casey and smiled, her small, even teeth shining in her face like pearls. "Has he forced you to sit through Woody Allen's complete oeuvre yet?"

"Are you kidding me?" Phoebe deadpanned. "They couldn't make it through the first five minutes of *The Rocky and Bullwinkle Show* without making out."

Sophie giggled around her straw, slurping her iced latte like someone was going to rip it away from her. Casey laughed nervously, but couldn't help noticing that Madison was staring at the floor—and rapidly shredding her paper napkin between clenched fingers.

"I know," Sophie said, turning to Phoebe. "I get a chronic case of third wheel-itis whenever they're around."

"Sure," Casey broke in good-naturedly. "Just talk about me like I'm not here—it's okay . . ."

"Well, at least we're not talking about you behind your *back* . . ." Phoebe grinned slyly and swept the crumbs of her muffin off of the table and onto the floor. "*Yet.*"

Phoebe and Sophie broke into a fit of giggles, and proceeded to slap each other a noisy high ten. Although she still had her shades on, and was still busily shredding what was left of her napkin into something the rexies might consume for a light snack, Casey was sure that behind those dark lenses Madison was rolling her green eyes in annoyance. In truth, Casey was feeling kind of conflicted about her newly minted couple status. Even though Mad and Drew weren't exactly "together" when Casey hooked up with him that night at his party, she knew Mad well enough at this point to realize that there was no way she could actually be happy for her. Madison Macallister had an ego the size of the tiniest yacht in the Hamptons—which was to say humongous.

But what bothered Casey even more was the thought that she might have turned into one of "those" girls—the kind that blow their friends off to hang out with some random guy. The kind that practically glues her cell to the palm of her hand, and checks her e-mail a hundred times a day—*and* her MySpace for any new messages. Ugh. She had officially become a teen cliché. Casey drained the last of her raspberry Italian soda and pushed the cup to the side, resting her elbows on the table. Had she magically turned into a backstabbing boyfriend stealer overnight, the kind of girl she used to loathe? And, worse yet, did she care enough to do anything about it?

"So what's the 411?" Sophie turned to Casey while exasperatedly pushing her bangs from her face, and reached into her bag with one hand, pulling out an amber prescription bottle. She popped the top off and placed a pill nonchalantly into her mouth, swallowing hard. "Or are you guys keeping things on the DL for now?"

"Are you *still* taking Adderall?" Madison asked with astonishment. "I thought you stopped seeing that shrink months ago."

Sophie blushed deeply and looked down at the table. "I did. I mean, I still see her sometimes. It's no big deal." Sophie bit her bottom lip and threw the prescription bottle back into the depths of her bag.

"Whatever," Phoebe interjected with obvious impatience. "We were *talking* about Casey and Drew. So," she said, a wicked glean animating her deep blue eyes. "What's the deal?"

Madison gazed at Casey impassively, waiting for her to speak.

"We're just . . ." Casey's voice trailed off as she tried to think of an appropriate yet descriptive way to explain what was happening with her and Drew. Lust was the one word that immediately sprang to mind.

"If you say 'friends' I'm going to vomit," Phoebe blurted out as her cell phone began to beep and buzz frantically again.

"Okay, that's it." Madison leaned forward on her elbows and removed her shades. Her green eyes swept over Phoebe, who looked up from the screen of her iPhone, a guilty expression crossing her heart-shaped face, her peaches-and-cream complexion flushing like vanilla ice cream mixed with strawberry. "Who the hell has been texting you all day?"

Phoebe threw her phone into her tote, and began gathering up her books. Casey didn't know about everyone else, but to her at least, Phoebe looked rattled and nervous as she tucked her French book under one arm and stood up, throwing the length of her dark, silky hair over one shoulder.

"It's my *mom*, okay?" Phoebe said crankily as her phone began to buzz yet again from the confines of her bag. Madison raised one eyebrow in what Casey was beginning to see was her signature move, and crossed her arms over her chest without answering. "She's so annoying lately."

"Tru dat," Sophie quipped as Phoebe reached into her bag and pulled her phone out again, staring at the screen, her brow furrowed. "I mean, aren't they *all*?"

"I've got to take this," Phoebe said, beginning to walk

away, her voice as rushed as her footsteps. "But I'll see you guys later, 'kay?" As she walked quickly toward the door, Phoebe raised her phone to her ear and began to speak, her voice hushed and secretive. "Hey, yeah, I can't really talk right now. Wait. Let me go outside . . ."

Casey watched openmouthed as Phoebe practically ran out of the dining hall. At the rate she was moving, she was probably creating enough friction with her cashmere-coated legs to send the school up in flames.

"What's *her* problem?" Sophie said, stealing the last chunk of Phoebe's forgotten muffin, her brow furrowed. "Too many Diet Cokes again?"

"Yeah." Madison laughed, gathering up her trash. "That girl's cuckoo for Cocoa Puffs."

"Well, whatever's going on, she's a total basket case lately—have you noticed?"

Madison nodded, inspecting her nails, but offered no comment. Casey just shrugged. It wasn't like she really knew Phoebe that well in the first place—she'd only been in Manhattan for six weeks—she could still barely navigate the subway without getting ridiculously lost, much less figure out the intricate workings of Phoebe's brain. And out of all the girls, Phoebe struck her as the most difficult to crack. While Madison's bitchiness was an obvious defense mechanism designed to keep people at a distance, Phoebe struck her as quietly, politely closed off. She seemed like the kind of person who not only had a lot of secrets, but who made it a habit not to share them easily either. Every time Casey tried to ask Phoebe anything even vaguely personal, she'd usually blink her incredibly long lashes a few times, then change the subject.

"So, what are you two lovebirds doing tonight?" Sophie asked, tucking her clutch under one arm and standing up. Casey blushed, gathering up her dreaded Algebra books and pushing her chair away from the table.

"He wants to take me to some Russian restaurant after school to eat blinis or something." Casey shrugged again, trying to act like it was no big deal. Madison pulled her shades off and slid them into her bag, which was trimmed with so much fox fur that it resembled a small pet.

"Oh, hell to the NO," she moaned, rolling her eyes up so far in her head that Casey was sure they'd get stuck. "Don't tell me he's taking you to the Russian Tea Room—it's so FTO!" Sophie and Madison cracked up, throwing their heads back in tandem so that their straight, silky hair swung down their backs. Noticing her confused expression, Madison leaned in, an amused expression enlivening her green eyes, and enunciated every word: "For. Tourists. Only."

Casey's cheeks flushed red as she followed Madison and Sophie out the door and into the hallway, blinking back the tears filling her gray eyes. Every time she felt like she was on the verge of fitting in at Meadowlark, some random, unforeseeable incident would invariably put her right back in her place—which just happened to be light-years away from the glamorous world of the Upper East Side. Casey sighed heavily, twirling a curl around one finger as she watched Madison lean over and whisper in Sophie's ear. Casey bit her bottom lip and attempted to focus on the sudden pain as her sharp teeth bit into her tender flesh as she tried to keep from crying. What did it matter if she was dating the hottest guy in school—in all of Manhattan maybe—if she always felt like an outsider?

As usual, and without even trying, Madison had won again.

welcome
to the
real world

Drew walked into room 14C, his pulse still jumping from
the touch of Casey's lips as much as from the anticipatory excitement of meeting Paul Paxil, the visiting filmmaker who
would be taking over his AP Cinema class for the next six weeks.
Paxil had catapulted to indie stardom two years ago when his
low-budget documentary *Blue Blood* won accolades at Sun-
dance, garnering massive critical acclaim and glowing reviews
when it opened at the New York Film Festival a few months
later. *Blue Blood* investigated the unsolved murder of a teenaged
socialite, Miranda Dime, in an affluent town in upstate New
York, and consequently succeeded in not only unmasking the
killers, but in reopening the case. His gritty, in-your-face documentary style landed him a three-picture deal with Miramax,
and his first big-budget feature, a courtroom thriller starring

Naomi Watts and Denzel Washington, had recently wrapped in London.

Paxil was not only a critic's darling, he was also a former graduate of Meadowlark Academy, and showed his pride by donating a pair of gleaming editing bays that hugged the far side of the room. He was also rumored to be the cash behind the school's plans to have 14C outfitted as a proper theater—with plush velvet theater seats to complement the sixteen-foot screen that dropped down from the ceiling with the touch of a button. Unfortunately, Paxil was also known as a bit of a diva and enfant terrible—recent articles in the tabloids linked him with Hollywood A-listers like Keira Knightley, Kirsten Dunst, and the Olsen twins, and lately his behavior had been described as more eccentric than professional by those who knew him best. Still, it hadn't exactly stopped the dean of Meadowlark from offering him a six-week guest lecturer spot in the fall curriculum.

Because of Paxil's celebrity status, the room was packed, and as a result, Drew had to walk slowly around the perimeter for a few moments, looking for an empty chair before finally spotting one at the back of the room. The large classroom was painted a warm beige, one wall lined with long, rectangular windows framed by plush window seats—a Meadowlark trademark—filled with an array of soft, brightly colored cushions. The room was buzzing with the sounds of furtive whispering and giggling, the excitement palpable as the door swung open and Paul Paxil walked briskly to the front of the room. Black jeans, black sweater, and black, thick-rimmed glasses, he looked like a classic hipster auteur. Part *I don't give a fuck* and part *everything I'm wearing is tremendously expensive, but I'd never let on to it.* And maybe just a dash of *I kissed the Olsen twins last night—both of them.* Just from looking at him, Drew wasn't sure if he wanted to hate him or if he wanted to be him. Maybe it was both.

"Just look at all of you," he said, instantly killing the chattering flowing back and forth around the room—even the Madison-ites of the room broke away from their iPhones and nail polish and looked forward, falling instantly silent. "A bunch of overprivileged, Upper East Side, cashmere-wearing sweater monkeys," Paxil sneered, the corners of his lips curling in disdain. "Well, we're going to fix all that," Paxil went on, waving a hand in the air and pacing back and forth unsteadily at the front of the room, the soles of his black Converse high-tops squeaking as he moved. "This semester you're going to grow something called a social conscience—and you're going to do it by making a thought-provoking, politically informed, short documentary film, exploring the subject of your choice."

Jenna Baumgarden, a petite brunette who made it a point to always sit in the first row of every class she attended in order to ask as many questions as she could possibly squeeze in during a sixty-minute class, raised one hand tentatively in the air while shaking back her mane of artfully streaked bronzed hair. Paxil nodded curtly in her direction. "Yes?" he snapped. "You have something you'd like to add?"

"Well," Jenna began, smiling weakly, "I'm not really political by nature. In fact I don't really think that—"

"It sounds like you don't really think—period," Paxil snapped, sitting down on the edge of the desk with a sigh and wearily crossing one black-denim-clad leg over the other. Jenna opened her mouth then closed it again like a guppy in a fishbowl, then rolled her eyes at Maria Chase across the aisle, who mouthed the word "asshole," her cherry-red lip gloss glinting in the light. "What I'm trying to do this semester, folks," Paxil continued, oblivious to the dissension that was forming in the room with every word he spoke, "is to get you to see beyond the boundaries of this suffocating little world you've created for yourselves."

Yeah, right. Drew thought, fighting back the urge to laugh out loud. Who did this guy think he was? Everyone knew that Paxil had grown up on Ninety-sixth and Park, and now lived in a humongous loft in Chelsea—he wasn't exactly living on food stamps or pawning his iPod for cash. He was making big-budget Hollywood movies and wasting millions of dollars in the process. The situation was so ridiculous that the laugh Drew had been stifling suddenly burst from his lips. As soon as it happened, Drew knew it was a mistake and tried to disguise the fact that he'd just laughed in Paul Paxil's face by coughing loudly, but it was way too late.

"Yes?" Paxil glared at him. "In the back—you, there." Drew exhaled as the whole room turned around to face him. "Is there something you'd like to add?"

"Not really," Drew mumbled, staring down at the smooth wooden surface of his desk.

"Am I so amusing that you feel the need to burst into hysterics during my class?" Paxil walked up the aisle and stood in front of Drew's chair, his eyes behind the high-concept glasses narrowing slightly.

"Kind of," Drew said quietly, as the room broke into a series of loud giggles and whispers.

Paxil leaned over and stared Drew down. He was so close that Drew imagined he could see every individual hair of the dark stubble on Paxil's jaw, so close that he now knew that Paxil smelled like coffee, chalk, and Issey Miyake cologne. "Your name is?" Paxil barked, straightening up.

"Drew Van Allen," Drew said tentatively, wondering what fresh hell awaited him now that Paxil possessed this all-encompassing information. Drew watched as Paxil spun on his heel and walked back up to the front of the room, sitting back down on the edge of the desk, his shoulders slumping dejectedly beneath his black sweater.

"So, Mr. Van Allen thinks I'm a hypocrite." Paxil sat there blinking thoughtfully from behind his thick lenses. It was a statement, not a question, and the room fell silent, waiting for Drew to either protest his innocence, or flip the pretentious asshole the bird, and stomp out of class. But before Drew could say or do anything, Paxil continued as though he'd never expected a response in the first place. "Well, he's probably at least partially right. I was a hypocrite—just like every one of you sitting so comfortably in this class. But I did something about it."

Yeah . . . you immortalized a dead socialite on celluloid, Drew thought to himself, making sure to keep his laughter from escaping once again, *that's not exactly negotiating peace in Darfur . . .* But he had to admit, regardless of how ridiculous Paxil might look in his general-issue, hipster film-snob fatigues, spouting his high-and-mighty bullshit, there was something to be said for the fact that Paxil had admitted his shortcomings. Not many people could actually stand up in front of a group of people and do such a thing, and knowing the demographic of the room he was sitting in, Drew figured that Paxil was probably the only one within a ten-mile radius that could and had. *But could I?* Drew thought, the laughter suddenly gone. *Maybe the only difference between us is the fact that he can admit it—and I can't.* Drew furrowed his brow and stared down at his desk, turning a pen over and over between his fingers, lost in thought. It really was a serious question—serious enough that Drew almost didn't want to know the answer. But wasn't not wanting to answer it an answer in its own right? He wasn't sure—but this whole film thing suddenly seemed a hell of a lot more interesting. Drew looked up as Paxil pulled John Anderson out of the front row and began deconstructing his wardrobe.

"Is it impossible," Paxil yelled, "to buy one article of clothing these days without a label plastered all over it?" Anderson, a tall, blond, exceedingly preppy guy who would probably asphyxiate without a plethora of alligators and polo-playing ponies to keep him company, cracked a nervous smile, blushing deeply and shoved his hands deep into the pockets of his dark brown cords. Drew rolled his eyes in sympathy, but inside he was beginning to wonder if Paxil didn't have a point. It wasn't like Drew was about to go run downtown and buy a pair of black 501s just yet—but maybe he *was* ready to get real, to give the act of examining his own life an honest, wholehearted try.

hello,
sailor

Phoebe held her long dark hair from the nape of her neck with one hand, cursing herself silently for forgetting to put a barrette into her tote this morning before she left for school, her other hand clasping her sister Bijoux's six-year-old fingers as she swung their hands manically back and forth, screaming, "Wheeeeeee Pheeeeebs!" with every third step of her black patent leather Mary Janes. At least once a week Phoebe made it a point to give the nanny the afternoon off and pick Bijoux up from one of the many dumbass activities Madeline was constantly scheduling for her youngest daughter. Today it was Mommy and Me class at the Gifted Children's Center of New York—except Madeline had never even bothered to show up. Thankfully, the Center was located just one block up from Meadowlark Academy on East Eighty-sixth Street, so when her cell rang, Phoebe had quickly raced up the block to collect Bijoux, whose impish face broadened in delight at the sight of her older sister. Phoebe watched as Bijoux kicked a pile of orange leaves with her tiny patent-leather-clad feet, screaming happily as the flame-colored leaves flew into the air. Even though it was the first week in October, the weather had become strangely, inexplicably warm, the balmy temperature belying the leaves strewn across the lush emerald-green grass of Central Park.

Phoebe knew she could traverse the Park blindfolded if she had to—it was as much a part of her as the tangled hair on her head, or her own two feet that took her closer and closer to the boat pond—the site of countless picnics and daydreams. In fact, she couldn't even walk past the pond without flashes of her sixth birthday party streaming through her brain—Mad and Sophie with cake in their hair and wooden boats in their tiny hands, the rustle of wind on the pond, the brightly colored miniature sailboats floating gently on the rippling water . . .

She rounded the gently curving path, every step taking her further away from The Bram Clan and Meadowlark Academy, the sparkling surface of the water reflecting against the lenses of her enormous bronze sunglasses, her heartbeat quickening as she spied Jared's lanky frame perched on the ledge surrounding the circular pond. He was anxiously tapping one blue and yellow DC sneaker against the pavement, his arms crossed over the beat-up army green Triple Five Soul cargo jacket he wore over faded jeans. Bijoux announced their arrival, yelling a chorus of what sounded like, "ME me me me ME!" at the top of her small but powerful lungs. At the sound of Bijoux's voice, Jared turned around to look at Phoebe, nodding nonchalantly at their approach as one hand came up and pushed his mass of straight, dark hair from blue eyes that could only be described as electric. Small clusters of kids Bijoux's age and younger ran around the perimeter of the pond, their small arms flapping with the sugar-crazed glee that only came from ingesting incredible amounts of candy and Popsicles—and subsequently running away from their nannies every chance they got. Phoebe knew that there probably wasn't a more neutral place to meet up in all of Manhattan than the boat pond, and she'd brought Bijoux with her as added insurance. So why did she feel so scared all of a sudden?

Phoebe took a deep breath and she willed her feet to move forward as she asked herself for the twentieth time just what the hell she was doing there. *He's your best friend's brother,* she told herself sternly, her feet moving relentlessly forward like she was being drawn in by a tractor beam—or some other sci-fi bullshit that her fourth-grade boyfriend would've probably known about. It wasn't like she hadn't tried to avoid him, but Jared was doggedly persistent. Ever since Drew's party, Phoebe had received a barrage of sexy e-mails and instant messages on a daily (sometimes hourly) basis. Not to mention the phone calls and text messages at all hours—including lunch. Phoebe knew all too well that if Jared's manic quest continued, it could really screw things up—especially if Mad decided to be her usual bossy self by grabbing the phone mid-text. Just thinking about it made Phoebe's nervousness suddenly take a backseat to queasiness, as her stomach began to toss and turn along with the brightly colored boats in the pond. And Sophie absolutely *hated* her brother—if she ever found out what had almost-kind-of-been going on lately between them, Phoebe knew that Sophie would never, ever forgive her.

"Can I go play with them, Pheebs?" Bijoux demanded, pointing at the other kids milling around the pond while tugging on the bottom of Phoebe's white sweater. "Okay, Beebs," Phoebe said sternly. "But stay where I can see you, 'kay?"

"YA!" Bijoux yelled, running off like her emerald green Petite Bateau pinafore and matching sweater was on fire. Phoebe turned to Jared, trying to force her face into a smile that seemed to come out more like a grimace, squared her shoulders, and prepared for battle. *The only reason you came here today,* she told herself, *is to tell him to knock it off, that you will never go out with him. Never.* "Just keep telling yourself that," she muttered, tossing her winter white, wool trench down on the stone ledge of the pond as she sat down next to him, pushing her shades on top of her head, the fall sunlight shifting through the trees, casting long, leafy shadows on the pavement. Jared turned to her and smiled, his blue eyes glowing in his still suntanned face.

"Hey you," he said, knocking her with his elbow, a wry grin plastered over his face. Phoebe felt her heart leap in her chest at his touch. *Here we go,* she thought, and exhaled heavily.

"I didn't think you would show," Jared said quietly, kicking one foot against the pond's cement rim.

"Me neither," Phoebe muttered, pulling her shades down over her eyes to avoid his gaze.

"But I hoped you would. And I'm really glad you came—even if you did bring a chaperone." Jared looked at the ground with a half-smile, then took her hand in his own, gently squeezing her fingers.

Phoebe was shocked at how good it felt to have her hand in his. His manly-looking paws were uncharacteristically soft, the smooth, firm touch of his flesh catching her totally off guard. He made holding hands as important as it had been in second grade when she'd walked to school with the then love-of-her-life, eight-year-old Marvin Jackson, who had grabbed onto her hand like a king-sized candy bar and didn't let go until they arrived at school, her fingers sweaty and slightly numb.

"I only came because you and I really need to talk," Phoebe said, her mind snapping back to reality after a mere second of Sophie's visage floated in front of her hand-holding fantasy land. She pulled her hand away and tucked it between her knees, hoping that it would be, somehow, out of Jared's reach. "This," Phoebe went on, "whatever *this* is—which is nothing. This nothing, or something—or whatever—needs to stop. Now. You're Sophie's brother and Sophie is my best friend and this absolutely *cannot* be happening. *Isn't* happening."

"Uh-huh." Jared nodded, that so totally cute and *completely* disarming smile making another appearance, brightening the entirety of his slightly salt-cured and perfectly tanned face.

"Yes. Uh-huh is right. And I guess that's all we really need to say about it," Phoebe replied, trying desperately to be all business, to resist the black hole of his hotness. Jared didn't reply, just kept on with that smile, his hand inching ever so slowly back toward her own. "Well then, I guess I'll be going," Phoebe went on, eyeing his slowly advancing hand as if it was a deadly spider, but one whose venom would bring her ultimate pleasure before death. She watched it and watched it, moving closer, moving faster, moving so completely and so obviously against everything she had just said that she found it impossible to take her eyes off of it. His hand found hers and she flinched, imagining the poison of his touch, the betrayal that such a simple action defined. She had to leave. Now.

"Wait. What were you saying?" Jared said, tightening his grip, his voice slow and relaxed, as if he had just awoken from a nap. "I was too distracted by the pretty that's all over your face—you should be more careful about that, you know. Getting pretty all over yourself—it could get you in a lot of trouble."

Despite her resolve to stay strong, Phoebe felt her face cracking into a smile. Like she wasn't in enough trouble already? Her life practically defined trouble as it was. *You have to leave,* she told herself. *Get up and just* go. Phoebe knew that if she stayed there another minute longer, she wouldn't be able to stop herself from touching him, or, God forbid, she might even *kiss* him—and that would be disastrous. Just the thought of Jared's smooth, red lips touching hers made her head swim like the fleet of blue and yellow boats dotting the surface of the pond.

Phoebe glanced across the pond, her dark eyes searching for Bijoux—who was currently straddling a little boy wearing a pair of dusty overalls and a blue cardigan. Bijoux sat on his chest, her little legs on either side of his flailing body, and appeared to be trying to shove a wooden sailboat up his nose. "Stay still!" Phoebe heard her sister scream out with no small amount of glee. "This won't hurt a bit!"

"I have to go," Phoebe said, throwing her bag over her shoulder and standing up, her tone conveying a decisiveness she *wished* she actually felt.

"Yeah. Me too." Jared stood up and stretched his arms overhead like a cat stretching in the sun. As she turned to walk away, he caught her arm, pulling her back. "Oh, just one more thing," he said with a half-smile on his lips.

Phoebe rolled her dark eyes in exasperation. "*What?*" Phoebe knew that she was in trouble. She knew that she should leave— hell, she should run, but her feet were curiously stuck to the pavement, and she found herself unwilling to wrench herself away from his grasp. Without another word, Jared pulled her to him, and as he leaned in, her senses flooded by the clean scent of his soap and that salty, citrusy scent that clung to his skin like seaweed, she couldn't stop herself from responding. It was like one of those dumb action movies where you see a car crash in slow motion. From somewhere that felt far way she watched as his head tilted toward her, felt a rush of salt wind as his lips touched hers, then the soft pressure of his mouth—powerless to stop any of it from happening.

Or, at least that was what she told herself as she leaned into his body, twining her arms around his neck, her soft leather bag dropping off her shoulder and onto the pavement as she closed her eyes and kissed him back.

tea
and
caviar

Drew leaned across the table and smiled, taking Casey's cool, slightly freckled hand in his own. Even though he'd been to the Russian Tea Room—in all its past incarnations—more times than he could count, here with Casey everything looked suddenly different: the heavy red velvet drapes that fell to the floor, the brass buttons on the waiter's black coat shining in the deep crimson light of the room, even the crystal-laden chandeliers hanging from the ceiling sparkled as if he was seeing them for the first time. Ever since he started dating Casey, he seemed to feel like this all the time, whether it was showing her his favorite Pollack at the Met, or introducing her to the simple pleasure of a hot corned beef on rye in the dingy yet supremely comforting dining room of Katz's Deli—the very fact of sharing these things with someone who got excited about them, too, was a whole new experience. One he could get addicted to if he wasn't careful. So far, at least, there was nothing about this girl that he didn't like.

Not that she was perfect—in fact, that was kind of the point. Casey was as far from conventionally flawless as you could possibly get, which by default *made* her perfect. Drew watched as she dug her fork into the plate of caviar and perfectly cooked blinis, holding back her mane of curls that went every which way with one hand, and raising the fork to her mouth with the other. Just looking at the way she parted her lips, closing her eyes as the tiny black fish eggs exploded on her tongue made him slightly crazy. He wanted to drag her under the pristine white tablecloth and do decidedly unculinary things with that gleaming silver boat of pillowy white sour cream . . .

"I always crave blinis in the fall," Drew said, his voice sounding almost as happy as Casey's tongue after her first taste of beluga caviar. "My dad took me here around this time every year when I was a kid—never in the summer or the spring or the winter—just the fall. I guess I'll never be able to make it through the month of October without a few fish eggs popping against the roof of my mouth."

"Who could blame you," Casey said between bites, her wide eyes clearly voicing her mind's wish that blinis were the size of vinyl records instead of silver dollars. "Although I think restricting the eating of caviar to the fall is a mistake—I could eat this stuff every day for every meal. Breakfast, lunch, *and* dinner."

"Then you and my dad will definitely get along well," Drew said, biting into the pillowy dough. "And that would be to your advantage, because if you want to eat caviar every day of the week, you're going to want to buy it wholesale—and he can. You know, this stuff costs hundreds of dollars a tin. They don't call the miracle that is caviar, lobster, and eggs a million-dollar omelet for nothing."

"Hundreds for a *tin?*" Casey said, looking at the little black pearls on her plate in a whole new light. "That's craziness. Maybe I'll stick with your whole once-a-year thing after all."

"It's a good system," Drew said, leaning back against the banquette and taking in the velvet-soaked luxury of the room. Madison had always refused to go to the Russian Tea Room with him. Having been forced to spend endless society lunches and birthday parties in this red velvet room since she was a child, she thought the place was total yawnsville—the type of old-school haunt where Edie and her friends went to drink vodka and knit quilts, or whatever the hell people her mother's age did for fun. "But most people who live in this city don't eat a normal person's paycheck for their breakfast," Drew said, motioning to the shiny, black eggs that spilled out of the plump pile of blinis on his plate. "I'm in this AP Cinema class this semester, and I think I'm going to make a documentary about it. Maybe interview the homeless or something," he said, stabbing another blini with his fork. "It's pretty awesome—Paul Paxil is taking over our class for the next six weeks, so I'm feeling like I should do something more socially conscious."

"Paxil?" Casey mused thoughtfully, the light glinting off her springy yellow curls. God, he loved her hair—it was like her curls had declared mutiny on top of her head and were planning a revolution. Drew was sick of everything that his perfectly groomed little world represented, and dating Casey was another way to widen it, to get his own hair messed up again—just the way he liked it. "I heard about his documentary but it never made its way to Normal, Illinois. Shocking, I know." She smiled, gesturing with her fork. "What's he like?"

"He's . . . intense," Drew said, punctuating his thought with a slurp of lemon-infused water. "And kind of an asshole."

Casey laughed, covering her mouth, which was full of sour cream and fish eggs, with one hand. "Big surprise," she said after she'd swallowed hard, wiping her lips with a white linen napkin before picking up her fork again, clearly considering what she was about to say next. "Why don't you make a film about something you've *experienced*—you know, first hand?" Casey's brow was wrinkled in thought, and she looked so god-damn cute that Drew thought he might have to drop his fork and sit on his hands for a while, just to keep from touching her.

"Like what?" Drew asked, trying to concentrate on her words instead of what was currently going on in his pants. He loved that Casey didn't just agree with him so they could move along to the next topic—she seemed genuinely interested in what he had to say. It was a nice change of pace from Madison, who made it a point to never listen to anyone but herself.

"What about making a film about being rich? You *definitely* know something about that."

Drew popped a bite of blini into his mouth and chewed thoughtfully. "I don't know," he said, swallowing hard. "I only moved up here two years ago—I mean, I never felt like I had all that much in common with those kids. I didn't grow up with all this." Drew pointed at the room with his fork before plunging into another blini.

"Are you kidding?" Casey said slowly with amazement. "You're friends with all of them!" Casey blushed hard, her face pinkening the way it always did when she felt like she'd said too much. "I guess so," Drew said grudgingly, studying his plate, a small smile hovering around his lips. "But my family definitely didn't always have the kind of money we have now—or at least we haven't always *acted* as if we did."

"But just because you didn't grow up with all this"—Casey raised her fork, painting a circle in the air with the shiny silver tines to make her point—"doesn't necessarily mean that you're not like them *now*, does it?" Casey asked tentatively.

"I guess I really don't know," Drew said, conceding the point, the smile sliding from his face, and the dark of his pupils deepening in thought. "At the end of the day, there's probably no more money in this room than there is in the dining room of, say, WD-50. The difference between downtown and here is *how* you spend your money—how you show it. I mean, my life hasn't all been champagne and caviar—but it could've been. My parents just don't really function that way—they're more from the $300-haircut-that-makes-you-look-like-you-just-crawled-out-of-bed school of being wealthy. And that shit doesn't really fly here. I see some of these people walking around with their custom-groomed teacup rat dogs with handmade Italian leather collars stuffed into five-thousand-dollar tote bags and think—know—that they're completely insane, that no one should be spending that much money on stuff like that. But I'm sure some people would look at my life, at my family, and think the same thing. I mean, let's be real—I'm not exactly chucking it all away to go work for Oxfam, or adopting a pack of Ecuadorian orphans any time soon. So, maybe I should try to figure it all out, you know? *Am* I like everyone else up here?" Drew took a sip of water, his mouth dry from his admission, his pulse thudding loudly in his ears.

Casey put down her fork and ran her fingers around the rim of her water glass thoughtfully. "Well, not everybody can be Angelina Jolie," she said with a smile that illuminated her serious gray eyes. "But you're right—you *should* figure it out. And making a documentary would be really awesome. I mean, who better to do it than you since you've seen both sides of the fence, right?" Casey's eyes lit up as she considered the possibility, and Drew leaned slightly forward, resting his elbows lightly on the table.

"You think?" he answered, reaching across the table and taking her hand again, tracing delicate patterns on her palm with the tips of his fingers. When she closed her eyes and sighed at his touch, he wanted to jump across the table and kiss her until they were both deliriously flinging sour cream everywhere. Somehow, he managed to control himself.

"I think," Casey said, opening her eyes and smiling, her gray eyes crinkling at the corners adorably. "Definitely."

"Maybe you could help me," Drew said, reluctantly letting go of her hand so that he could take another bite of rich, caviar goodness.

Casey shrugged her shoulders and looked confused as she ate the last bite on her plate and chased it with a sip of water. "I don't know anything about making a documentary," she said, blotting her full, naturally red lips with a white linen napkin.

That was another thing he really liked about Casey—he didn't have to claw through layers of goop just to kiss her. Mad had worn so much makeup that making out with her had sometimes felt like kissing one of those perfume inserts in *Vogue*—totally artificial. "Playing the violin is the only thing I've ever been good at," Casey said, a wistful note coming into her voice.

"I didn't know you played the violin," Drew said with surprise, leaning across the table and grabbing the salt, sprinkling it delicately over the tender, boiled potatoes that circled the edge of his plate. "How long have you been playing?" Drew could barely contain his excitement. Just when he thought he'd heard it all, Casey gave him yet another reason to like her even more than he already did.

"Since I was six," Casey said with an audible sigh. "But since I've moved here, well, not so much anymore. I used to think that I wanted to try to get a chair in a symphony somewhere, someday. But now I'm not so sure." Casey looked down at the tablecloth, tracing invisible patterns on the spotless white fabric with the tip of her index finger.

"Will you play something for me sometime?" Drew asked, his mouth full of potatoey goodness.

"If you want." Casey smiled, her face flushing pinkly.

"And, by the way," Drew said, swallowing hard, "I don't know much about it either—making a documentary, I mean. I have a pretty high-end Canon that my dad got for Christmas a few years ago and I've cut some random footage in Final Cut, so I know the basic tech stuff. But you could help me set up the shots, write the interviews—you know?"

"Okay," Casey said excitedly as the waiter cleared their plates, her eyes shining. "It sounds like fun."

"Will there be anything else, sir?" The waiter stood there, pen in hand, as Drew stared across the table at Casey, their eyes locked on one another, and Drew found himself mesmerized by the way her gorgeous lips were beginning to curve into a smile.

"I hope so," Drew said, still staring at Casey. "Definitely."

meet your
new
mommy

Sophie St. John threw a heavily distressed denim mini-
skirt with a rip up the side to the floor of her plush, electric-violet
carpeted closet, and sighed audibly. It was official—even after
the relentless shopping she'd been doing lately as an attempt to
wage warfare on her parents' credit cards—the financial equiv-
alent of a professional hit—she *still* had nothing to wear. Ratio-
nally, Sophie knew that her closet was stuffed to the point of
ridiculousness with the best Fifth Avenue had to offer, but there
was just nothing she felt excited about—and that made the act
of getting dressed each morning seem like a chore rather than
the total delight it should've been. Sophie pulled out an Isaac
Mizrahi green-and-blue plaid skirt circa 2002, and stared at it
in horror before kicking it behind a pile of weathered Coach
monogram luggage piled against one lavender wall.

Truth was, she hadn't been excited about anything really since her parents broke the news about her adoption. After the initial euphoric high had worn off, depression had set in, and now she felt more lost than ever. Being her usual bright, bubbly self at school was really starting to take a toll—acting like you didn't have a care in the world, when in reality you felt like you were carrying Trump Tower on your back, was completely exhausting. At first she'd been beyond excited about the prospect of finding out exactly who her bio mom was, and maybe even meeting her face-to-face. But now she wasn't so sure how she felt—about anything.

From deep inside her closet, she heard the unmistakable sound of knuckles rapping lightly on her bedroom door, and, in exasperation, threw the pair of black suede Fendi boots she was holding to the floor before answering. "Come *in*," Sophie shouted, her tone matching her mood as she stomped over to the door and flung it open. Her mother, Phyllis St. John, stood in the hallway, a manila envelope in one hand, her face flushed and anxious. Phyllis had obviously just returned from one of her biweekly tennis lessons as she was clad in a demure, white Ralph Lauren tennis skirt with a matching cashmere tank, a cherry red sweater tied casually across her toned shoulders. Sophie wondered how her mother was able to play tennis for two hours straight and stay so spotless—not to mention sweatless. It was a complete and total urban mystery. In fact, someone should get the CSI team to swoop in and figure it out—pronto.

"Can I come in?" Phyllis asked, looking worried that Sophie might say no and slam the bedroom door in her face. And, although the thought *had* crossed her mind, Sophie shrugged her shoulders and opened the door wide, stepping away from the doorway and back into the womblike interior of her closet. Her mother stood there in the center of Sophie's lavender room, tapping the envelope against one tanned leg, shifting her weight uncomfortably, her dark hair pulled back in a neat twist.

"So, what's up?" Sophie asked as she plucked a vintage Zandra Rhodes tunic in light pinks and yellows that positively swam on her from a hanger, and threw it at the discard pile. Phyllis sat on the bed, absentmindedly running her hand over the violet and slate blue silk comforter with one hand and crossing one slim thigh over the other.

"I have some information for you," Phyllis said quietly, then cleared her throat noisily before continuing. "About your . . . mother." Sophie walked out of the closet and stared at her mother. It sounded so completely *Twilight Zone* to hear her mom describing someone *else* as her mother. The effect was totally disorienting, like something in her brain had shifted violently. Sophie looked at the manila envelope that Phyllis was nervously turning over in her hands.

"Is that it?" She gestured at the envelope, her mouth suddenly crazy dry.

"It's everything you need to know," her mother said with a sigh, her shoulders slumping as if she'd been rapidly deflated, a pained expression crossing her unlined face courtesy of bimonthly Botox injections, thank you very much. "If you *want* to see it, that is." She held out the envelope hopefully, her platinum and sapphire eternity band glittering in the light.

"I *guess* I'll take a look," Sophie said, trying to sound like she didn't care. But on the word "look," her voice cracked, and she almost burst into tears. As her fingers closed around the smooth paper, she had to concentrate hard, fixing her eyes on her typed name on the label affixed to the front so she didn't break down. There was no way she could handle crying in front of her mother right now—the whole thing would just turn into some teary mother/daughter bonding experience when all Sophie really wanted was for Phyllis to leave the room so that she could read about her bio mom in peace. It felt way too personal to share with anyone else—even the woman she'd thought of as her own flesh and blood for almost sixteen years.

"Well, I have to meet your father for dinner, so I'd better get changed," Phyllis said with forced brightness, averting her blue eyes from her daughter's face and walking briskly to the bedroom door. Sophie could feel her mother's pain—it was practically sucking all the oxygen out of the room—but she felt helpless, like there was nothing she could do about it. Sophie had spent most of her life so far putting other people's feelings before her own—but for some reason she just couldn't do that now. Even for the person who had raised her, who she was supposed to love more than anything. *But maybe that's the point,* Sophie thought as she watched Phyllis walk stiffly out of the room. *She's not my mother. Not really.* But what made someone a mother anyway? Was biology absolutely *everything?* Maybe she was placing too much importance on some random collection of eggs and sperm . . .

As soon as the door closed behind her, Sophie sat down on her bed, staring at the envelope in her lap, and trying to breathe regularly as she contemplated opening it. She hadn't cut herself since her parents had told her she was adopted, and, at times like these, it was really hard not to simply walk into the bathroom, pop the blade in her razor from its casing, and dig into her own flesh until she cried tears of relief. What she missed the most about cutting was the calm that followed, how she'd feel all quiet inside herself, ready to move on to the next disaster. Nothing about her life was calm anymore, but since she hadn't run to the bathroom yet, she supposed the combination of going to therapy when she felt like it and meds was finally helping. Sophie put her index finger in her mouth and began to gnaw on her nail instead. That stupid fucking envelope was like Pandora's box—once she opened it, nothing in her life would ever be the same again. *But things are already different*, she thought as she took a deep breath, running her hand over the slick paper, the sharp edge slicing the tip of her index finger. *And even if I don't open it, there's no going back.*

Sophie opened the envelope and stared blankly down at the eerily familiar face of an attractive woman in her late thirties, Sophie's own honey blond hair cascading past her shoulders, and bottle-glass green eyes shining in her angular face. As Sophie perused the rows of typed information, her mouth fell open in shock when she arrived at the name written at the bottom of the sheaf of legal documents: Melissa Von Norton.

"Holy crap," Sophie whispered as she traced a finger over the smooth contours of her mother's face. Melissa Von Norton was one of the most highly recognizable and respected actresses in Hollywood—more Meryl Streep than Julia Roberts—who was known for her relentlessly angelic beauty, as well as her penchant for accepting roles in gritty, independent films. She'd even been nominated for an Oscar one year, but lost out to Dame Judi Dench in the final moments.

Sophie closed the envelope and sat on the edge of her bed in shock. Whoa. This was big—bigger than she'd ever dreamed possible, and there was no way she was going to be able to keep it a secret anymore. She had to talk to somebody. And *fast*.

Sophie grabbed her phone and opened her call list. Madison was definitely out. At least until she knew more—like whether or not her mother even *wanted* to see her. With that thought, a spasm of fear wracked Sophie's heart, squeezing it with cold fingers. How could she *not* want to meet her own daughter? It was kind of like asking how a mother could possibly give birth to a child, then give it away without a second thought. Sophie shivered, her spine convulsing with the idea. Better not to think of that now—or she'd never go through with any of what she was about to do.

Phoebe, as much as Sophie loved her, would only end up blabbing to Madison. Pheebs possessed a lot of admirable qualities but, unfortunately, keeping secrets wasn't one of them. It totally sucked, because Phoebe was exactly the kind of listener she needed right now—quiet, attentive, and usually pretty helpful. Why didn't she know anyone *else* like that? Sophie furrowed her brow and gnawed on the nail of her pinky finger, effectively destroying what was left of her manicure. Was there anyone she could count on to be completely impartial, to not blab to everyone at Meadowlark? Sophie's eyes widened as she opened up her text messages, her fingers flying over the slick surface of her iPhone.

Can u come over?

Now?

Yeah. Busy?

No! Be up in a sec.

Sophie signed off, and opened the envelope again, her eyes transfixed on the serene planes of her mother's celestial face as she waited for Casey's knock at the door.

a
model
life

Madison strolled down her favorite stretch of pavement
on the entire Upper East Side—Madison Avenue, the street she
was named for—her cognac-colored Gucci boots clacking on
the sidewalk like the hooves of the sleek Arabian horses she
used to jump when she was eleven. She remembered waking at
the ridiculous hour of six A.M. to run out to the stables in the
park and ride through the sun-dappled paths for hours, the
wind in her then naturally platinum hair, the clicking of hooves
on the well-traveled paths ringing in her ears. Madison sighed,
pushing her white-blond hair behind her ears so that it wouldn't
get caught in the MAC Lipglass that coated her full lips in the
most delicious, iridescent rose-gold sheen. Things were so much
simpler back when she spent her time falling in love with horses
instead of boys . . .

Madison stopped in front of Prada, mesmerized by the truly bizarre window display that featured several bald, naked mannequins surrounded by stuffed wolves, black alligator bags hanging from their thick, furry necks. *Why would you need wolves to sell purses?* Mad thought, taking a sip of the iced vanilla latte she held in her left hand. *Why wouldn't you?* her inner fashionista answered soberly. *Good point*, she thought, smiling at the red, lolling tongues hanging out of the furry creatures' mouths. A soft tap on her shoulder shook Madison from her couture-dominated reverie, and she spun around, startled. A tall, dark-haired man in his late twenties stood in front of her, a smattering of five-o'clock shadow decorating his impossibly square jaw, his dark eyes boring into her own.

"Scusi," he said apologetically. "I did not mean to disturb you. I was hoping to ask you a question," he added softly in lightly accented English.

"Yes?" Madison said, still a little freaked out, her adrenaline pumping through her veins in a rush that felt vaguely illegal.

"Are you a model, by any chance?"

Madison laughed, relieved that he wasn't some random, totally gorgeous psychopath. He was just horny, and in Madison's, albeit limited, experience horniness made guys do stupid things—like walk up to total strangers and annoy them with a bunch of dumb questions. "No," she said, throwing her hair back as it whipped around her face in the cool breeze. "I'm not."

"Well," he said, his smile revealing rows of straight, white teeth that shone in their close proximity to his olive skin, "would you like to be?"

"That depends." Madison angled her body closer and smiled coquettishly. "Who are you, anyway?"

The dark-haired hunk of gorgeousness in front of her held out his hand apologetically, and bit his full lower lip sheepishly before answering. "My name is Antonio Phillipe—I am a scout for Verve Model Management." Madison took his hand, which was so large that it made her giant man hands feel tiny by comparison. That was the worst thing about being tall—everything about her was larger, including her Jolly Green Giant–sized hands and feet. Whenever she had to shake anyone's hand, she practically broke out in hives from the fucking stress of it all. "Perhaps you have heard of us?" Antonio inquired, still clutching her hand like it was an inflatable raft and they were lost at sea.

"Of course," Madison said, trying to come off like she met scouts from world-famous modeling agencies every day of her life. Verve had represented Cindy Crawford at the absolute height of her career, *and* Naomi Campbell, aka, The Body—or the phone-wielding lunatic, whichever you preferred. Standing there with Antonio's hand in her own gargantuan paw, Madison had the feeling of absolute rightness, the sense that some great destiny was being fulfilled right there in the middle of the traffic and bustle of Madison Avenue. And why shouldn't it? After all, she had, in one way or another, been preparing for this moment for her entire semi-adult life. Now it was here—and she wasn't about to blow it. Not by a long shot.

"Let me give you my card," Antonio purred, reaching into the inner pocket of his black Hugo Boss blazer and removing a silver monogrammed card case. He snapped it open with a flourish of the wrist, and handed her an embossed business card, his dark eyes holding hers until she thought her knees might buckle. "A woman like you is too beautiful to be walking down the city streets—you should be on a runway with men falling at your feet, the best photographers in the world capturing your every move."

Damn straight, Madison thought, taking the card between her fingers and dropping it into her Furla tote, praying to God that it didn't get lost among her endless credit card receipts and Trish McEvoy makeup brushes. *This guy is definitely cheesy—but good*, she thought, moving the hair from her face so that it flowed down across her back. Antonio definitely had game—Madison doubted that Drew could pick up a girl so effortlessly. Drew was cute, but Antonio was . . . hot. And hot completely slayed cute any day of the week.

"Thanks," Madison said, trying to look both humble and totally irresistible at the same time.

"Call me," Antonio said, pointing an index finger at her before walking away.

"Maybe I'll do just that," Madison murmured under her breath, transfixed by the yummy sight of Antonio's perfect ass framed by dark washed jeans. Madison floated down the street in a daze, her boots barely touching the pavement. It was all going to be so perfect she could barely stand it. By Thanksgiving she'd be gracing the catwalks of Manhattan, Paris, and Milan—she'd have a hot new career and an even hotter new boyfriend. High school boys were so totally last year . . . Even so, she couldn't help smiling smugly as she pictured the look on Drew's face when her glowing visage showed up on the cover of

Vogue—or when Antonio picked her up in front of Meadowlark for their first of many dates, a red rose in his hand . . .

No—red roses were a total romantic cliché. Madison stepped into the cool perfumed interior of Barneys, scanning the makeup counters with a practiced eye. He'd be wearing a dark suit, and holding a spotless, white African daisy . . . Madison wandered over to a glass display of imported men's cologne, spraying the testers liberally. The Acqua di Parma cologne that lingered in the air above her head filled the store with a lemony freshness, and fairly reeked of warm Mediterranean sands and the Italian Riviera—just like Antonio.

Madison sprayed herself liberally with the citrusy scent, and exited the store, blanketed in the summery, lemony musk. This was going to be the best year ever—not only would all eyes be on her, as usual, but those eyes would include most of the entire *planet*. Look out world—Madison Macallister was about to become a household name, which was unarguably better than just being somebody's girlfriend. Besides, Madison knew from experience that revenge was sweet—but success was bound to induce a diabetic coma.

And Drew Van Allen was in for the sugar shock of his life.

poison ivy

"Phoebe, darling, is that you?"

Madeline Reynaud's voice rang out through the foyer just as Phoebe stepped through the front door of the Reynauds' apartment, the stiletto heels of her black leather boots clicking jauntily on the Italian marble floor as Bijoux let go of her hand and ran screaming across the foyer and into the kitchen.

"Sebastian," she called out to their Parisian chef, who, from the mouthwatering scents of roasted meat wafting from the kitchen, was busy making dinner, "I want coooooookies!"

Phoebe frowned, throwing the white wool Tahari trench she carried over one arm onto a polished oak credenza that hulked in the front hall, and tossing her Tod's cream leather tote on top. "Yes," Phoebe called out tiredly to her mother, stopping in front of the sterling silver starburst mirror that graced the foyer wall, staring at her reflection in the shining glass. "Coming." Her cheeks were pink from the chilly outside air, and her eyes glowed in the soft, amber-and-bronze colored lamplight drifting through the apartment from her mother's extensive collection of rare Tiffany lamps. She was lying to one of her best friends—shouldn't it show? "You're a fake," she murmured to herself. "A fake and a liar. Just like your mother."

"Phoebe!" Madeline's voice rang out again, this time with a decidedly exasperated note. "Will you *please* come into the living room *maintenant*? There's someone here I'd like you to meet."

Phoebe rolled her eyes and walked toward the sound of her mother's excited chatter. The Reynaud living room was almost unbearably formal, decorated with lumpy, overstuffed furniture and lots of spindly, gilt-edged little chairs that Phoebe was always nervous to actually sit on—and for that reason it was hardly ever used, except for the rare occasions when Madeline wanted to impress someone. A glittering seventeenth-century French chandelier hung from the ceiling, the sparkling crystals drawing attention to the elaborate crown moldings that were painted the color of fresh cream. A black and crimson rug dominated the large rectangular room, partially covering the shining mahogany hardwood floors underfoot. Madeline and an unfamiliar woman were perched on the larger of the two overstuffed sofas in front of the white marble fireplace, shimmering crystal flutes of champagne clutched in their hands, their heads huddled together, their whispers echoing in the cavernous room. Despite the unseasonably warm temperature, white birch logs snapped and crackled happily on the hearth, filling the space with the cheerful, autumnal scent of burning wood. As Phoebe walked in, Madeline looked up, her blue eyes bright with champagne and excitement. Phoebe knew that combination well, and it made her suddenly nervous.

"This," Madeline said, twisting her wrist to point toward the stranger in a slow, practiced arc, her gold Cartier Love bracelet sliding in languorously toward her bouclé blazer the exact hue of crushed cranberries, "is Andrea Cavalli, the best personal college admissions coach in Manhattan."

Phoebe quickly gave the woman a once-over: smart, well-fitted clothes—beige, red, and black Burberry Nova Plaid skirt, and snug, black cashmere blazer, thick, black hair pulled back neatly into a ponytail, square glasses with black rims sitting on the bridge of her nose, and sensible-chic red Ferragamo pumps with a wooden stiletto heel. A gold Tiffany charm bracelet tinkled on her wrist as she pushed the black frames up on her tiny nose. She was nondescript, but in a way that was subtly aware of being so—as if everything she wore, every groomed strand of hair and patch of skin was the way it was for a definitive purpose. It was an artful nondescript. *If this were a movie,* Phoebe thought to herself, *this woman would definitely be cast as a hardcore assassin—like Uma Thurman in* Kill Bill—*except you wouldn't see Andrea coming until it was way too late.*

"Phoebe—a pleasure," Andrea said, rising from the couch and reaching out her perfectly manicured hand—clear nail polish—to shake Phoebe's, whose nails were lacquered in Chanel Vamp, a deep purple-blackish retro shade that Andrea, she somehow knew, would immediately notice. And take note of.

"Andrea," Madeline said, her voice practically purring with

pleasure, "is going to get you into Harvard. And you're going to do whatever she says—no questions asked."

Andrea smiled broadly, and sat back down, crossing her legs, which produced a whooshing sound when one thin, silk-stockinged thigh grazed the other.

"Phoebe," Andrea began, patting the overstuffed crimson loveseat and waiting for Phoebe to sit down. Phoebe walked slowly over to the sofa and plopped down with a sigh, folding her arms over her chest. Like her life wasn't awful enough right now? Apparently not. Surely what she really needed was some overgroomed college drill sergeant telling her exactly what to do every day of her life until the end of senior year. The thought was almost enough to make Phoebe run screaming from the room, pack her bags, and run away somewhere hot and laid-back—like Brazil, for instance. "The SATs are coming up—fast—and we really need to whip you into shape in preparation. Of course," she added, turning to Madeline, the lenses of her spectacles shining in the lamplight, "test scores aren't the only thing admissions will be looking for—especially when it comes to an Ivy. Do you have any extracurricular activities we can play up on your application?" Andrea stared at Phoebe eagerly, waiting for her to respond.

Extracurricular activities? Phoebe thought wordlessly. Unless Andrea counted making out with her best friend's brother like a crazed monkey and power shopping as activities, Phoebe knew she was probably out of luck. And from the eager expression on Andrea's tight, pinched face, Phoebe already knew without being told otherwise that these weren't the kinds of answers she was probably hoping for.

"Not really," Phoebe mumbled while furiously chipping the polish off her thumbnail.

"I see," Andrea said frostily, turning to Madeline conspiratorially. "Well, it's definitely clear why you need me." Andrea pulled a black leather Hermès notebook from her Burberry tote, flipping through the pages. "Desperately," she muttered distractedly as she unclipped a Montblanc pen from the notebook, and began to scribble furiously on the unlined, white page. "Now I recommend that Phoebe and I meet at least once a week—with two or three phone sessions thrown in for good measure, and there's always my daily focus e-mails as well—to keep her on track. It's so *easy* these days for young people to become *distracted*," she added, smiling thinly at Madeline, who began to nod sympathetically, her pearl drop earrings from Van Cleef & Arpels pulsing whitely in the light.

Phoebe's mouth fell open. *Kill me,* she thought, glaring at her mother, who ignored her, as usual, and continued to gaze at Andrea approvingly. "Does Dad know about this?" Phoebe asked her mother, her eyes narrowing. "It seems like there's *a lot* he doesn't know lately."

"Your father and I have discussed it," Madeline answered frostily, reaching up to pat her dark, shining hair, which was smoothed back in a French twist. "And he agrees that you are *clearly* in need of some direction."

"I *have* direction," Phoebe snapped. "I'm going to be a fashion designer—remember?"

"I'd prefer not to," Madeline said dryly, flashing Andrea an exasperated smile. "You're going to Harvard Business School just like your father—it's all been decided."

Phoebe felt herself deflate like the delicate chocolate soufflés at Le Cirque once you stuck a fork in them. Like every other girl in Manhattan, and probably the entire planet, Phoebe loved clothes. She adored everything about them—the way rough tweed felt under her hands, and the whisper kiss of the softest cashmere grazing her ear. Last winter her grandmother had taken her to the fall collections in Paris, and it remained the most exciting moment of Phoebe's life. At the Dior show, the clothes swirled down the runway with a life of their own, the silk and brocade gleaming in the bright, white lights. At the end when John Galliano himself stepped onto the runway, blowing kisses at the audience as he pranced down the catwalk, Phoebe jumped to her feet and clapped furiously, tears springing to her eyes. At that moment, she wanted more than anything for her designs to grace that runway someday, to see a young girl in the crowd clapping excitedly over *her* creations. But if she was forced to go to Harvard Business School and spend her days in marketing class, and her nights making spreadsheets with Excel, Phoebe knew she'd probably never get the chance.

"We'll start next week," Andrea said, standing up and brushing off her skirt with one hand as if she'd been sitting on a hay bale instead of a twenty-thousand-dollar antique sofa with Baroque scrolled legs and gilt edging. "I'll send you an e-mail with all the details sometime tomorrow, Phoebe," Andrea said briskly, grabbing a Burberry trench from the arm of the sofa and throwing it over her arm like she was stanching a wound.

"Let me walk you to the door, Andrea," Madeline purred, standing up and straightening the hem of her nubbly cranberry Chanel skirt, the heels of her black Manolo Blahnik ankle boots tapping the hardwood floors like Morse code as they exited the room and moved into the hallway without so much as a backward glance.

Phoebe tried to fight the tears that were welling up in her blue eyes. She felt small, like her whole life had been shrunk down to fit perfectly in a tiny Kate Spade clutch, her dreams squashed to fit her parents' unrealistic expectations. She felt like things were moving too fast lately, getting more complicated when all she wanted was for things to be simple—they way they used to be before she fell for Jared, before her family began to fall apart. As much as she wanted her life to slow down and just *stop*, it seemed to be speeding up faster and faster— whether she liked it or not.

And Phoebe knew that if she wasn't very careful, it wouldn't be long before her entire life became someone else's, and her future spun completely out of her grasp.

secrets
revealed

Casey plopped down on Sophie's bed, kicking off her scuffed, cream-colored Old Navy ballet flats, and grabbed one of Sophie's oversized down pillows, hugging it to her chest like a teddy bear. "So, what's up?" she asked, momentarily resting her cheek against the cloudlike surface. God, Sophie's pillows and sheets were so supremely soft that she wouldn't have been surprised if Sophie had informed her they were fashioned from the tender skin of newborn babies. Maybe that's why high thread counts were so ridiculously expensive . . .

"Okay, before I start, you have to promise that you won't say anything—to *anyone*." Sophie sat down on the bed next to Casey cross-legged, leaning her elbows on her knees. Sophie wore a pair of butter-soft cashmere sweatpants in bright orange, and a plain white wifebeater with a rip in one shoulder strap. Even in her casual clothes, Casey couldn't help noticing that Sophie was still stupidly pretty—which would've usually intimidated Casey to the point where she froze up and became unable to put words together like a normal human being. But despite her good looks, Sophie was the one member of The Bram Clan around whom Casey felt almost comfortable. There was something about Sophie's wide-eyed grin and easy playfulness that made Casey feel like she wasn't existing perennially on the very fringes of coolness, ready to topple into the abyss of loserville at any second. Around Mad or Phoebe, Casey felt like she always had something stuck in her teeth, or that her hair was threatening to branch out and take over the planet. With Sophie, she felt like it might just be okay to simply kick back and be herself.

"Sure." Casey threw the pillow to the floor and crossed her legs, mirroring Sophie's pose exactly. "Who would I tell, anyway?"

Sophie stared at Casey like she'd eaten a brain tumor for breakfast and rolled her green eyes, giggles sprinkling her words like nuts on a sundae. "You never know what might, ahem, 'slip out' in the heat of passion . . ."

Casey picked the pillow up off the floor and threw it at Sophie, who ducked it cleanly, smiling wickedly. Nothing was in danger of "slipping out," though she'd rather bury herself in the noxious, gray cement they were using to repave Fifth Avenue than admit that to Sophie, but it was true—things between her and Drew were definitely not at the slipping out—or in—level yet. They were definitely getting there with every lingering, delicious kiss—but it wasn't like they spent hours ripping off each other's clothes every day after school or anything. *Unfortunately for you*, her inner dating Nazi snapped.

"I mean it," Sophie went on, her face solemn. "You really can't tell anyone—*especially* not Mad."

Now Casey was *really* intrigued. Why would Sophie rather confide something so obviously important in her, and *not* the girls she'd known for her entire life? With uncanny accuracy, Sophie read the confused expression that must've been all over Casey's face, and continued before Casey could even begin to verbalize her question.

"I can't tell them—not yet anyway. The reason I'm telling you is because I *haven't* known you forever. You know?" Casey nodded, though she still wasn't sure exactly what Sophie meant. Sophie raised her arms over her head, pulling her streaky, honey blond hair back in a messy bun and securing it with a tortoiseshell clip plucked from the violet carpet, which stood out in sharp contrast to the lavender walls of Sophie's bedroom. *Maybe*, Casey thought, *I don't know anything about fashion—or interior design—but it kind of looks like Barney threw up in here . . .*

"So . . ." Casey said, leaning forward. "What's going on?"

Sophie took a deep breath, picking up a manila folder at the foot of the bed and opening it across her lap, her hands placed strategically over the contents. "A few weeks ago my parents told me that I'm adopted," Sophie said quietly, her voice emotionless, her gaze level and direct.

"Oh my God," Casey murmured. "Are you okay? I mean, what did they *say*?"

Sophie looked away, blinking rapidly. "Oh, some bullshit—apparently they were having problems getting pregnant after my idiot brother was born, so they adopted me as some sort of deranged consolation prize for *not* going through a round of IVF." Sophie took a deep breath and let it out slowly, still looking away.

"Wow. Umm. *Wow.*" Casey felt like she'd suddenly become a drooling idiot—in the blink of an eye, her whole vocabulary reduced to a rapid succession of one-syllable words. The problem was that she just didn't know *what* to say. What was the correct response to something this personal and deep? "I'm sorry" didn't exactly sound right, and "bummer" definitely wasn't going to cut it.

"And that's not all," Sophie continued, moving her hands away from the open manila folder and placing it in Casey's lap. "Look," Sophie said, pointing at the photograph pinned to the top of the thick sheaf of legal documents. "That's *her*. My mom."

Casey stared down in disbelief at the face in the photograph, goosebumps popping up on her arms. "Melissa Von Norton's your *mom*?" Casey looked up at Sophie, her mouth falling open. "I saw *Playback* in the theater five times last year!"

"Me too," Sophie said, staring down at the photograph, seemingly lost in thought, her fingers tracing the planes of her mother's face. "I can't believe I never noticed the resemblance—though I guess you never really go around looking for your own face in anyone else's." Sophie leaned back against the immense pile of pillows that were mounded up at the head of her bed. "My mom knows her—if you can believe that—they were in the same acting class together when my bio mom was just starting out. They were friends—a long time ago."

"Are you *serious?*" Casey asked, unable to keep the amazement from her voice. Casey looked into Sophie's eyes, noticing immediately that they were the exact same shape and color as her biological mother's—and that Sophie also looked dangerously close to crying. "Sophie, that's just *crazy,*" Casey said softly, mostly because she just didn't know what *else* to say.

Casey sat there for a moment in the silence that had fallen over the room, winding a curl around her index finger, and wondering how it would feel to wake up one day and find out that your whole life had been a lie. Casey stared at Sophie, who was busily picking loose threads from her comforter, her face set in rapt concentration. *She must be so lonely right now,* Casey thought, reaching out to touch Sophie on the shoulder. Sophie jumped like she'd been burned by Casey's touch, and gave Casey a weak smile. "So," Casey said, removing her hand, trying to bring the conversation back someplace vaguely practical. "What are you going to *do?*"

"What do you mean?" Sophie took the folder back and closed it, tossing it to the floor.

"I mean you have to *call* her or something!" Casey bent over and grabbed the folder off the floor and opened it again. "Or meet her. Isn't there a number for her in here?"

"No." Sophie sighed, pointing an index finger at the bottom of the first page and tapping it with her nail. "Only an e-mail address."

"Then you have to e-mail her!" Casey exclaimed, grabbing

the folder and walking over to Sophie's MacBook, sitting down at her white lacquered, ultra-mod desk.

"Hang on," Sophie cautioned before Casey's hands could so much as hit the keys. "I don't even know if she wants to hear from me—much less see me!"

"Then isn't it time you found out?" Casey asked, turning to face Sophie, who had her arms crossed over her chest defensively. "Come on," Casey said softly, reaching out and touching Sophie's arm. "This is your *mom* we're talking about—don't you want to *know* her?"

Sophie opened her mouth, then closed it, biting her bottom lip as she mentally weighed the pros and cons of making such a ballsy move. That was the thing about e-mail—once you let your words loose in the unruly world of cyberspace, you could never really take them back or, more important, delete them.

"Does she want to know *me* is the question," Sophie muttered, releasing the clip from her hair so that it fell down around her shoulders.

"And why *wouldn't* she?" Casey retorted. "You're her daughter, aren't you?"

"I guess," Sophie mumbled while inspecting her nails, neatly avoiding Casey's eyes. Casey wasn't sure exactly why Sophie was so hesitant to contact her mom—especially now that she was practically Hollywood royalty. Casey knew that if she was ever lucky enough to find herself standing in Sophie's shoes, she'd be sitting on a plane, sunglasses on, faster than you could hum the opening bars of the theme from *The O.C.* "Come on," Casey said decisively, running her hands over the mouse and waking up Sophie's sleeping computer. Just as she opened

Sophie's e-mail, Sophie sighed, pushing her over on the chair.

"Shove over and let me do it," Sophie said bossily, strategically pushing her butt onto the chair so that Casey's own butt cheek was suddenly hanging fleshily—not to mention precariously—in the air. *Why does my butt have to be so big?* Casey lamented silently, noticing the way Sophie's entire ass fit neatly on the small space—along with Casey's half-cheek. Sophie's ass was so small that you could probably fit two of them neatly side by side on the matching white lacquer surface.

"What are you going to say?" Casey wondered aloud as Sophie's hands flew over the keys, her eyes focused on the white screen.

Dear Ms. Von Norton,
My name is Sophie St. John, and I have just been informed that you are my biological mother . . .

"My sweet sixteen party is coming up, right?" Sophie said, her fingers still typing furiously. "I was thinking about maybe inviting her."

"Umm . . . Do you think that's a good idea?" Casey asked, trying to be tactful. In truth, she really couldn't think of a *worse* idea. Way to put pressure on the entire night! Not only did Sophie have to pull off one of the hottest parties of the year, she was going to meet her biological mother in front of four hundred of her closest frenemies? Throw in the fact that her mother just *happened* to be one of Hollywood's biggest movie stars, and you had the potential for a disaster of epic proportions—kind of like *Titanic*, but on dry land, surrounded by couture . . . "And why aren't you sixteen yet anyway?" Casey asked, changing the subject, her brow lined with confusion.

"I skipped the sixth grade," Sophie said with a shrug. "So I'm a year younger than everyone else. It's totally stupid." Sophie's hands stopped dead on the keys as she turned to look at Casey. "So, why *wouldn't* it be a good idea to invite her?" she asked nervously, catching her bottom lip between her white teeth. "I mean, it's only the most important night of my *life!*"

Exactly, Casey thought, groaning inwardly while trying her best to plaster an expression on her face that appeared both positive and supportive. "No reason," Casey said quickly, hoping she sounded appropriately cheerful.

"So, let's do it," Sophie said crisply, suddenly all business as she turned back to the screen, a determined expression on her face as she deleted what she'd written with a sharp click of her mouse, and started all over again.

From: ssj@meadowlarkacademy.com
To: starbaby@aol.com

Dear Ms. Von Norton (Melissa? Mom? Not sure what to call you),

This is a strange e-mail to write, and probably an even more random one for you to find in your inbox.

My name is Sophie St. John, and I have reason to believe that I am your daughter. According to my parents—and the files from the Tender Care adoption agency on W. Fifty-seventh Street—you gave me up for adoption on November 3, 1991, in New York City, where I still live with my parents on the Upper East Side. My "other" mother has told me you were in her acting class, and that you were close friends a million years ago.

There is so much I don't know about my life, things I think only you can tell me. I'm turning sixteen in a few weeks, and I'd love if you'd consider coming to my party. I hope my asking doesn't make you feel uncomfortable, but I'd really like the opportunity to sit down and talk with you—or, if that's impossible, an e-mail would be a good start ☺.

Sincerely,

Sophie St. John

lights,
camera,
distraction

Drew was only twenty minutes into watching the footage of his interview with Alexis Anderson, senior at Meadowlark and total hottie, and he already wanted to scream. Why was
every girl he interviewed so spoiled and self-obsessed? As he
stared at the screen, he quickly became aware that the movie he
had just begun making could very easily become feature-length.
He had spent a few hours the day before interviewing Alexis in
the living room of her parents' Park Avenue apartment, which
featured, among other things, fourteen-carat gold-leaf detailing splashed across the pristine, white moldings of the sixteen-
foot ceiling. It was the kind of apartment where you couldn't
touch the walls; where some chairs were meant for sitting on
and others where you just *thought* about how nice it would be
to sit in them. *I could just film the apartment, no interview at*

all, and that could be the whole movie, Drew thought to himself as he stared at the glowing screen of his MacBook. But as Alexis offered up another picture-perfect sound bite about remembering to say thanks after receiving a brand-new BMW Z3 coupe and a Cartier watch for her birthday, he quickly scratched that idea—this stuff was too good to be true.

Alexis was one of those girls that was so beautiful, so physically perfect that she seemed to exist in a completely different reality. It was doubtful that a single guy at Meadowlark didn't harbor some illicit fantasy that involved Alexis and her lightly toasted almond skin, disarming blue eyes, and her totally slammin' body. And that tooth. The tooth was, for some reason, the thing about Alexis that had always drove Drew's libido into overdrive. She had one crooked tooth that jumped forward when she smiled in a way that would be undoubtedly ugly on any other girl, but on Alexis, it served as some sort of seal of authenticity, like the little bubbles in Venetian handblown glass, imperfections that somehow had come to denote the utmost quality—and demanded the highest prices. And that was the image that Drew had always had of Alexis—the most perfect, sexy, beautiful, and expensive senior at Meadowlark. But as he looked at her digital likeness on the screen in front of him, he realized that he would never see her that way again—that tooth meant nothing to him anymore. After all, the whole reason he'd broken up with Madison was that she was just way too caught up in all the UES drama that came along with being young, rich, and living in the city's most desirable zip code. Even though Drew was pretty sure that Alexis was flirting with him all through their interview, the thought of dating her now was inconceivable. She was so egotistical and spoiled that she kind of reminded Drew of Madison on steroids—and if he couldn't handle Mad's own diva bullshit, hooking up with Alexis was totally out of the question.

"I feel that I'm, like, totally aware of the privileges I have. I mean, I go down to the Village to go shopping sometimes and I *see* the way people live down there. It's experiences like that that make me grateful for everything I have. And aware that there are other people that don't have this stuff." Alexis blinked rapidly onscreen as she responded to Drew's question about the income disparity in the world. And while he, like so many other New Yorkers, certainly thought of Manhattan as the epicenter of the world—if not the entire universe—he had been thinking more along the lines of differences between socioeconomics in the United States and Darfur, not the Upper East Side and the Village. *Is it really possible to be this completely uninformed?* Drew thought to himself as he marked the time code for that clip in his notebook and then pressed play again.

"I mean, poor people are just like you and me," Alexis said enthusiastically—always the humanitarian. "They just have less money." Drew rolled his eyes and hit pause. She was giving him so many priceless sound bites that he didn't even know which one to choose anymore.

"Drew, are you in there?"

The booming voice of Drew's dad, Robert Van Allen, was unmistakable, and Drew glanced at Alexis's still face on the screen one last time before answering, tossing his pen down on the desk. "Yeah," he called out, "come on in."

"Hey, buddy," Robert said as he stepped through Drew's

doorway wearing a food-splattered white chef's jacket and an ancient pair of ripped jeans, his knees poking bonily through the holes. Robert Van Allen was one of the most famous chefs in all of Manhattan, and his signature restaurants were continuously packed months in advance. After years of working back-breaking shifts, his dad was now mostly retired, and preferred to supervise from a distance rather than run his eateries on-site. But ever since the opening of his latest venture, Boudin, a Cajun-fusion restaurant, a few months back, he'd been coming home progressively later and later each night. "What are you working on?" he asked, sitting down on Drew's rumpled bed, and pushing aside the plaid flannel Ralph Lauren sheets that were scrunched into a ball at the foot of the bed.

"Just reviewing some footage," Drew said, the frozen image of Alexis, despite the utterly ridiculous words that had just come out of her perfect, pillow-lipped mouth, still making his jaw want to drop. Like in a cartoon.

"Reviewing some footage, huh," Robert replied, following Drew's gaze to the screen, "so *that's* what they're calling it these days," he deadpanned. "Do you need me to leave you alone for a while," he asked, fighting to keep a straight face. "This isn't one of those live, online camera chat things, is it?"

"No, Dad." Drew laughed, clicking to minimize the window. "It's for the movie I'm working on. You know, the one I was talking about with you the other day. About rich kids and our neighborhood and all that."

"Oh, *that* movie. I remember. How's it been going so far? Are all of your interviewees going to look like *that?*" Drew's dad asked, playfully knocking him in the shoulder with a loose fist. "That might not make this movie of yours very popular with that Casey girl."

"Actually, she's been helping me out with this thing. She wasn't along for Alexis's interview," Drew said, gesturing to the screen, "but she's been working with me on the writing and is going to give me a hand with the rest of the interviews, too."

"That's good to hear, Drew. Just keep an eye out for girls like Alexis here. If I'm not mistaken, you have a bit of a soft spot for the perfect, blond, model-looking type."

"I have no idea what you're talking about," Drew shot back, a bit too quickly. He was in no mood for one of his dad's heart-to-hearts—especially about girls. As much as he loved his dad, his advice was based on fairly obvious observations more often than not, and as a result, he was rarely the source of sage advice he believed himself to be. Especially when it came to girls. Which is exactly when he felt especially convinced that Drew *needed* the benefit of his experiences. Or train wrecks.

"Does the name Madison Macallister ring a bell? You know, the girl that you've been dating for the better part of the last few years?" Drew's dad quipped as he pulled the sleeves of the threadbare white chef's jacket he wore up to his elbows. He rested his bare arms on his knees, leaning forward. These were the telltale signs of an oncoming advice assault—it was his *Let me tell you something* stance. Drew braced himself. "What *did* happen with you and Madison? She never comes around anymore. And you've been spending an awful lot of time with that Casey girl."

"Stop calling her 'that Casey girl,' Dad." Drew snapped, unable to hide his annoyance. "I know her name. *You* know her name. It's Casey McCloy. And yes, I guess she might kind of be my girlfriend—or something like that. And, yes, Madison and I are history. And I just might like things better this way—that's about as much as I can figure out right now," Drew said, looking toward his dad, trying to get the facts out on the table and out of the way, hoping that they could get through this as quickly as possible.

Robert leaned over even farther, balancing his elbow on his knee and wedging his hand firmly under his chin, stroking his salt-and-pepper beard the way he always did while mulling over something complicated. "That's a lot of 'guesses' and 'kind ofs,' Drew. Doesn't sound like you're much too certain about any of this. And you maybe kind of think Alexis is really pretty and could sort of be your girlfriend, too, right?" His eyes lit up at the question mark, and the joy that this father-son-girlfriend-intrigue stuff brought him peered out from beneath the put-on air of somberness he tended to use during such conversations.

Shit. Drew exhaled heavily, staring at his father's expectant face. Drew realized there was going to be no getting out of this quickly—he was going to have to talk this one out with his dad, for better or for worse. "Yes, Alexis *is* gorgeous. So is Madison. But I think I'm tired of girls like that—girls that have everything and seem to be perfect. And I think I'm happier with Casey. She doesn't buy into all the stupid he said/she said bullshit that Madison and Alexis—and most of the girls uptown—are so obsessed with. You know what I mean?"

"I know exactly what you mean," Robert replied with a smile, leaning back against Drew's pillows. "You know, that's the way I felt about your mother when we first met. She was so beautiful and smart and so totally different from any other girl I'd ever known." Drew's mom was none other than Allegra Van Allen, a world-famous painter and art-world beauty. Even though they'd been married for over twenty years, his parents fairly panted with lust for each other on a daily basis. Ever since Drew was around six, he'd understood that when his parents disappeared into their room in the middle of the day to "take a nap," that other secret, stickier things were probably taking place. While other kids at Meadowlark lamented their parents' divorces on a regular basis, Drew felt smug and slightly superior in comparison—most of all, his parents' obvious devotion made him feel safe, like everything was right in the world of Drew Van Allen.

"Not that it made me give up on the other girls right *away*," his dad went on, clearly lost in his own memories. "She made them seem so different, too . . . different from her. But in the end, of course, you know how it all worked out." Drew's dad slapped his knees with the palms of his hands, got up, and headed for the door, pausing with his hand on the knob.

"Don't feel like you need to rush yourself, Drew—you don't have to have it all figured out right now. You're a young guy— play the field and have fun—that's what youth is for, you know."

Drew put his bare feet up on his desk and leaned back in his chair, his arms behind his head. "And you should know, right? I mean, since you're so old and everything . . ." he answered back, a half-smile on his lips.

"Proving once again that youth is *definitely* wasted on the young," his dad retorted with a snort as he closed the door behind him.

Drew turned back to the screen, his dad's words swimming around in his head, confusing him. What was wrong with being a serial monogamist? It had never felt right to Drew to simply go out with girls just because he could—it was so much more fun to really get to know someone rather than take them out, hook up, and never talk to them again. He didn't really see the point. And besides, it wasn't like he really wanted to represent some cliché of what a sixteen-year-old guy should be. Just because he was supposed to be ass-crazy all the time, just because his hormones were in overdrive twenty-three hours out of twenty-four didn't mean that he had to be a player. If you played, eventually you *got* played, and Drew wasn't interested in being just another conquest. Most of the girls at Meadowlark expected so damn much from a guy they were dating, and one of the things he loved about Casey is that she didn't expect *anything* from him—or anyone—and that made her appreciate what she got. For the first time, Drew was starting to see what it could feel like to want to give a girl everything you had—simply because she didn't demand it.

And it felt good.

strike
a
pose

Madison stopped before the frosted-glass doors leading to the offices of Verve Model Management and took a deep
breath, pulling out a gold Chantecaille compact, and blotting
her nose and cheeks with translucent powder that shimmered
slightly against her golden skin. School had been interminable,
her head filled with images of striding down the Versace catwalk in Milan, Antonio seated in the front row next to Dona-
tella, his dark eyes flashing more powerfully than the white lights
clouding her vision . . .

Except now that she was finally on the threshold of taking
the modeling world by storm, Madison was feeling just a smidge
more nervous than she would've liked to admit—not that there
was anything to be nervous *about* really. When she'd called Antonio the day after their encounter on the street, he'd told her

to come right in as soon as she could, the excitement in his voice crackling like static electricity. And besides, she was wearing her lucky outfit—a dark-washed pair of Joe's low-rise skinny jeans, and a black, wool Prada jacket with a black cashmere tank beneath, and Jimmy Choo pumps that were the absolute definition of hotness with shiny silver zippers running up and down the black leather. The entire ensemble screamed supermodel. So what did she have to be nervous about? This was destiny, and as far as Madison was concerned, her destiny was waiting just behind those frosted-glass doors—in the form of a scorchingly hot Italian guy with model good looks, and the connections to match. Madison pushed open the doors, tilting her chin confidently in the air.

The monochromatic gray lobby was filled with the bustle of ringing phones and the sharp sounds of stiletto boots tapping against the bleached wooden floors as assistants walked briskly by, their arms full of papers. A row of scarily gorgeous girls sat on a line of stiff-backed chairs, sleek leather portfolios cradled in their matchstick arms. Madison was no stranger to beauty—after all, she'd grown up with some of the most beautiful girls in Manhattan—but the polished, pampered exteriors of the Upper East Side's elite couldn't even begin to touch the otherwordly glossy veneer these girls were genetically blessed with. They were so strangely, hauntingly beautiful that it was almost unsettling to look at them for more than a few moments. *Did they manufacture them at a factory somewhere in Eastern Europe and ship them to New York when they turned fifteen?* Madison wondered nervously as she approached the front desk, clearing her throat softly.

The Amazonian blond receptionist—who possessed the most hollowed-out, sculpted cheekbones Madison had ever seen in her life—held up an index finger, a headset firmly strapped to one ear, her light gray, almost colorless eyes perfectly complementing the darker gray wall behind her, the shade of storm clouds. Just looking at her, Madison began to worry again—this girl was only the receptionist, yet she looked as if she'd just climbed out of one of the framed magazine covers adorning the gray walls and sat down behind the desk just for kicks. "Shit," Madison mumbled under her breath as the receptionist turned to her, her eyes sliding up and down Madison's body from face to feet with cool, practiced ease.

"Yes?" she deadpanned, a flash of amusement enlivening her formerly dead stare.

Madison drew up her shoulders and stared her back down, summoning all the confidence she could muster. "I'm here to see Antonio."

The blond gave her a half-smile, her eyes turning suddenly frosty.

"I assume you have an appointment?"

"Of *course*," Madison answered haughtily. All she had to do at moments like these was conjure up her mother, Edie, and it worked every time. It was a good thing, too, because when she'd talked to Antonio yesterday he'd told her to just come on down—she hadn't even thought to schedule an appointment. And besides, no one ever got anywhere by playing by the rules or making appointments. Rules were for wimps and losers—not glamazons-in-training.

"Madison, darling! You made it!"

Madison turned around to Antonio's smiling, Armani shades obscured his dark eyes. He walked up to her as if the wooden floors were made of butter, taking her hand in his own and planting a smooth, practiced kiss on her knuckles.

"How long have you been here?" he inquired. Before she could answer, he took both her hands in his own, holding her at arm's length, taking in the faded jeans that fit her every curve, and the fitted jacket that hugged her torso, squeezing her waist from negligible to nonexistent. "You are a vision, *cara,* an absolute vision!" Antonio wasn't looking too bad himself in dirty-washed Diesel jeans and a forest green T-shirt peeking out from beneath a chocolate velvet blazer. "Come with me to my office," Antonio purred, taking her by the arm. "We have much to discuss, no?"

"Definitely," Madison cooed, allowing Antonio to lead her out of the waiting room and down a long, carpeted hall that reverberated with the shrill sound of ringing phones. But before she exited the waiting room completely, Madison couldn't resist turning around and shooting the receptionist a satisfied smile, her green eyes flashing triumphantly. The receptionist smirked right back, her dark matte lips turning up at the corners lightly, before being distracted by yet another call ringing through her headset.

Antonio's office resembled a page out of an IKEA catalog— all sleek, Swedish modern furniture dominated by a white egg-shaped lamp that glowed brightly on his ebony desk—despite the late-afternoon fall sunlight streaming through the venetian blinds, casting horizontal patterns on the gray walls.

"Sit, *cara,* sit!" Antonio gestured at the horrendously

uncomfortable-looking steel and Lucite chair directly across from his desk. Madison sat, crossing one leg over the other, her heart beating so loudly she briefly went all Woody Allen—practically convincing herself that she was about to keel over in sudden cardiac arrest. She didn't know what made her more excited—the prospect of being a supermodel, or her proximity to Antonio. He was so totally yummy that she briefly imagined pushing the paper and portfolios that crowded his desk to the floor and pushing him down on top of the slick wooden surface, pulling his T-shirt up with one hand . . .

"So," Antonio said, removing his sunglasses with a smile, flashing his blindingly white teeth, "we must talk seriously of your career today. I will have my assistant take some Polaroids, and your measurements, *si?*"

"*Si,*" Madison agreed, positively giddy with excitement. God, when her adrenaline rushed like this it was almost better than drugs, and definitely better than sex—or at least the sex she'd had so far, which admittedly had been less than perfect. That horrible night she'd spent with Drew last spring began to miraculously fade from her memory as she watched Antonio pick up the phone, barking orders in a stream of rapid-fire, authoritative Italian before banging the receiver back in the cradle with the ringing of bells.

"And I will, of course, give you our contract to take home with you and look over. It is just a standard contract," Antonio said with a shrug as a pencil-thin brunette in achingly tight skinny jeans entered the room with a clipboard in one hand, a Polaroid camera in the other. "Nothing to worry about."

"I'll have to talk it over with my mom," Madison said nervously as the brunette motioned for her to stand up.

"Yes, yes," Antonio said with a wave as the phone began to ring again. "Have her call me if you like."

"Okay," Madison said as she stood up, the brunette wrapping a length of cloth measuring tape around her waist, smiling happily as she recorded the results on her clipboard, "I definitely will."

"We will set up your test shoot for sometime next week." Antonio picked up the phone, holding one hand over the receiver. "I will call you with the information."

"Test shoot?" Madison said breathlessly, as the tape—which was now around her breasts—was threatening to cut off her circulation entirely.

"With a photographer," the brunette clarified, her blue eyes as round as marbles in her pointy face. "To see how you photograph."

"I thought that's what *those* were for." Madison pointed at the Polaroid camera the assistant had placed on her vacated chair.

"The Polaroids are just for us," the brunette said briskly while picking up the camera. "To make sure you're not a total disaster on film before we spend money on test shots. Now, stand up against the wall and look straight ahead."

Before Madison had time to pose, the flash went off like a gunshot, colored spots spinning in front of her eyes, the photograph popping out of the bottom of the camera with a slick, grinding noise. The assistant waved the photo in the air, fanning herself, a bored expression on her fine-boned face.

"Why aren't you a model?" Madison asked while they waited for her likeness to appear on the empty surface. "You're pretty enough."

The assistant rolled her blue eyes, her voice dripping with sarcasm. "Yeah, right," she scoffed as she brutally slapped the nonexistent excess flesh of her legs. "With these thighs?"

Madison shrugged, but inside she shivered a little. This girl was just about flawless with legs like stilts, and she thought she was too fat? Madison frowned as the assistant fanned the photograph in the air again with one hand—the other still hovering obsessively around her thighs. Just what was she getting herself into here—a life of dieting and insecurity? *But that's pretty much the life I'm living right now anyway—without the added benefit of being famous*, she reasoned as the assistant stopped her manic fanning and stared down at the now-developed image.

"Wow—the camera loves you!" she exclaimed, shoving the Polaroid under Madison's nose.

Madison stared down at the photograph, transfixed, unable to believe that it was her own face looking back at her, the face she'd seen a million times in the mirror. Madison had always known she was pretty—there was no point in denying it or even in acting humble—but who was this girl with the razor-sharp bones in her face, those green eyes that gazed back at her like the embers of softly-glowing emeralds? So lost in her thoughts was she that she barely noticed when Antonio walked up behind her, staring at the photograph over her shoulder.

"Belissima," he purred, grabbing the photo from the assistant's bony fingers. "I think, *cara,* that you are going to be a

big, big star—and I am hardly ever wrong," he added, a flirtatious gleam enlivening his dark eyes.

Madison smiled back, her stilettos barely touching the
ground. She felt like she was floating somewhere over the Em-
pire State Building, her stomach a mass of turning, jumping
excitement tempered with a sense of calm that she couldn't
quite explain. This was it—her destiny had come to her as she
always knew it would. She smiled as she pictured both Drew's
and Casey's faces when she broke the news.

Of course, being a supermodel was definitely going to be
fabulous—that went without saying. But Madison had the
sneaking suspicion that making Drew and Casey suffer was going to be even better . . .

To: ssj@meadowlarkacademy.com
From: starbaby@aol.com

Dear Sophie,

I was overjoyed to receive your e-mail among the endless spam clogging my inbox! I've been hoping to hear from you for some time now—I'd even thought of contacting you myself, but I didn't want to intrude in your life in any way that might be unwelcome.

In response to your question, I'd love for us to meet. I'm shooting a film in Los Angeles with Paul Thomas Anderson right now, but it should wrap in time for your sixteenth birthday! Of course, I'd love to come to your party. I can't wait to get out of L.A.—if I see one more starlet carrying a tiny, sweater-clad dog, I just may lose what's left of my tiny mind ☺.

Can't wait to meet you—I know we'll have loads to talk about. Please give my love to Phyllis.

xoxo
MVN

get the
party
started

"What could she have been thinking?" Sophie said with obvious disdain, pointing at a photograph of a girl swathed in a poofy white marshmallow of a dress that looked as if it would be more suitable for a nine-year-old's ballet recital than a sixteen-year-old attending the biggest party of her life—it positively screamed New Jersey Turnpike.

"Well, *you* don't have to wear it," Sophie's mother, Phyllis St. John, said with an exasperated sigh as she smoothed her freshly blunt-cut dark bob with one hand, her diamond and emerald rings sparkling in the light as she obsessively crossed and uncrossed her long legs swathed in sheer, cranberry-hued silk stockings that perfectly matched her nubbly tweed Chanel suit.

"Thank *God*," Sophie snapped, closing the heavy, leather

photo album spread across her lap, and took a swig of her Diet Coke, sneezing as the bubbles promptly went up her nose. Sophie crossed her arms over her chest and looked around Randi Gold's tasteful, subtly chic black and white office.

Randi was one of Manhattan's premier party planners, focusing exclusively on upscale sweet sixteens that not only broke the bank, but usually left Daddy crying to his accountant. Towering over the competition at six foot four, and tipping the scales at well over two hundred and fifty pounds, Randi was a force of nature with a personality to match. He smiled at Sophie and Phyllis with lips that shone with just the tiniest application of sheer gloss, and smoothed down his pink and white–striped tie that perfectly matched his baby pink dress shirt with French cuffs, four-carat diamond cufflinks sparkling at his wrists. He smoothed back his close-cropped blond hair with a hand heavily laden with diamond rings. To Sophie, Randi looked like a huge, bloated, and blond Baby Huey—or a character out of Alice in Wonderland. She half expected his brother, Tweedledee, to come barreling through the doorway at any moment . . .

"Would you be interested in renting out some wildlife for the event?" Randi asked, pulling out a brochure from a private zoo upstate that leased exotic animals to film productions and the occasional ultra-lavish birthday event, his fingers like plump, pink sausages. "The ocelot has been exceptionally popular lately—it has that leopard style, but much more sleek, the pattern more refined."

"But aren't they . . . dangerous?" Sophie asked as she pictured herself walking into the party flanked by two totally muscular, bare-chested men walking a pair of ocelots that prowled across the floor, the cats shackled to long, silver leashes, the chains studded with intricate rows of Swarovski crystals.

"I guess they could be considered a bit of a liability," Randi said, rising from the sleek, sexy curves of his white leather office chair, the back of which was encased in a hard, reflective shell of perfectly smooth black fiberglass. "A girl lost a finger to one not too long ago," he went on, his voice conversational, showing no hint of concern. "But thank God she did—I heard the beast took a most hideous and garish diamond ring off with it. An animal that looks that good couldn't *help* but have a tremendous flair for fashion, wouldn't you say?"

Sophie shrugged and looked down at her own fingers, her perfect oval-shaped nails tipped with a smooth curving line of white. A thin silver ring holding a small but perfectly clear and exquisitely cut diamond sat on the first finger of her right hand. It was a far cry from a fashion violation, Sophie thought, remembering the day she went to pick it out with her mother (*supposed* mother, Sophie corrected herself) just after her thirteenth birthday. Nothing a fashionista jungle cat would want to do away with. But she certainly didn't want to run the risk— Sophie knew from experience that it was often the people with the most unfortunate taste who were the most intensely vindictive.

"I think we'll skip the ocelots," Sophie said, looking over to her fake mom, who was examining the rings on her own fingers, a far off look in her eyes.

"What about doves?" her mother said, looking up from her jeweled hands and back to the exotic animal farm brochure that

Randi had handed to her. "A whole flock of doves, flying out of cakes or boxes or vases as the guests all walk into the room. What about that?"

"Doves could be fun," Randi said thoughtfully, his hands floating over the elongated, curved paperweight that sat on his desk, which seemed to have been carved from a single, impressively sized and beautifully grained piece of ebony, mother-of-pearl detailing running along its top edge.

Sophie shuddered and shook her head quickly from side to side. Doves? White birds in general belonged at weddings and funerals—not fabulous, exclusive sweet sixteen parties.

"But how about flamingos instead?" Randi wondered aloud, his blue eyes glazing over dreamily. "A hundred flamingos flying around a swiftly flowing, pink-white blur of a room. You dressed in pink—but not cute little-girl pink," Randi said, his hands flying into action, each pale-skinned finger a lithe tropical bird, pecking its way through the pile of glossy brochures covering his desk. "I want you in something that's more high school sexpot meets elegant French colonialist. A hint of Indochina. The scent of jasmine." He flipped viciously through a thick three-ringed binder, Sophie's anxiety mounting by the second as someone's dream dress flew by with each turning page. Where was hers? The pages stopped, his hands finally relaxed. "This," he said, his voice full of ceremony, "*this* is the dress for your party; the dress for you."

His finger pointed to a cascade of pale pink chiffon that tumbled to a terrified-looking blond model's ankles like a cascade of bubble gum–flavored whipped cream. The dress had a huge, flouncing skirt, complete with a bright pink bow on the back. Sophie felt her face drain of blood as she stared down at the photograph. It didn't matter in the slightest that the dress was Valentino, or that it was a couture piece, it was, bar none, the ugliest dress Sophie had ever seen—and there was no way she was going to be caught dead wearing it on the most important night of her life. Sophie leaned forward and pursed her lips, resting her hands on her knees.

"Ooooh, it's absolutely darling!" Phyllis cooed, grabbing Sophie's arm excitedly. "Randi, you're an absolute genius!"

Randi blushed an alarming shade of pink that almost matched the horrific dress in front of them. Sophie stared at both of them incredulously. Had everyone gone totally psychotic? She'd look like a walking cupcake in that thing, a bridesmaid at some awful Long Island City wedding where the groom wore a white tuxedo and the cake was bought at a goddamn supermarket!

"Randi," Sophie began, trying to be delicate, "I don't think you really understand how important this night is for me."

"Honey." Randi laughed, showing off rows of teeth as white and large as tombstones. "I do four hundred of these parties a year *minimum*—I know *exactly* how important this night is for you."

"Randi," Sophie began again, trying to stay cool, "I don't think you're really listen—"

Sophie sighed exasperatedly as her mother's phone began to buzz violently from the depths of her caramel Birkin bag. Phyllis shot Randi an apologetic smile, flashing her new custom shaded veneers.

"Excuse me for a moment, you two," she said staring down at the screen of her metallic gold, D&G Razr while heading toward the door. "I simply *have* to take this."

As soon as the door closed, Sophie knew she only had a few minutes to make Pinkberry listen to reason. Sophie smiled enthusiastically, dropping her voice and almost whispering. "I don't know if my . . . mother mentioned this," she began in a tone of voice that suggested that she alone had the info to Brangelina's whereabouts at this very second, "but there is a serious VIP who'll be in attendance that night . . . someone very *important*." Sophie paused for dramatic effect, sitting back on the chair and crossing her legs.

The slightly miffed look on Randi's face slowly gave way to something resembling interest. *Way to be predictable*, Sophie thought, watching the greedy expression slide over his face. Everyone was such a total starfucker.

"I'm adopted," Sophie said, watching as the gossip-hungry look slid off Randi's face and was replaced by a gaze of obviously practiced sympathy. "And my biological mother is Melissa Von Norton."

Sophie watched as Randi's face changed from fake sympathy to total starfucker in a matter of seconds. "Melissa Von Norton the *actress*?" Randi said with obvious excitement. "Oh my God, I just *adored* her in *Pale Blue Sea!*" Randi's face flushed pinkly again, and he waved his hands in the air giddily, his heavily jeweled fingers flashing in the light.

"So, now you see exactly why this night is so special to me," Sophie explained as the door opened with a squeak, filling the air with the scent of Bond No. 9's Chinatown perfume, which always smelled to Sophie like a combination of flowery incense, and awful Indian takeout.

"Okay, I'm back," Phyllis said brightly, reaching over and placing a hand on Sophie's own, her face falling slightly when Sophie inevitably shrugged it off and tried to lean even farther away in her chair. "What did I miss?"

"Well, now that Sophie's filled me in on her . . . celebrity connections," Randi flipped the book in front of him closed with a flourish of his wrist, and stage-whispered suggestively, "I'm thinking of going in another direction altogether."

"Celebrity connections?" Phyllis asked weakly the color slowly draining from her expertly bronzed face. As she watched her mother's expression change from hopeful to a look that screamed utter despair, Sophie almost wanted to throw her arms around Phyllis and tell her that everything was going to be all right, that she forgave her. But the problem was the word "almost." Almost wasn't definitely, and, at that moment, Sophie felt anything but definite about the entire concept of family—much less ready to forgive her own.

"Sophie, here, has just informed me of her . . . parental situation," Randi said smoothly as Phyllis turned deep red and contemplated her fingernails. "And that got me thinking at a whole new, infinitely more fabulous level!" Randi stood up and began pacing back and forth excitedly. "What if we did something a little retro—but with a modern twist? I was thinking that, as a theme, we could revisit Studio 54!"

Sophie began to smile again. She loved anything retro or vintage, and Studio 54 had been the home of glamour and glitz all through the 1970s. And there were so many amazing designer options to choose from—she could already see herself draped in a Grecian-style vintage Halston gown, her face and hair sparkling with discreetly placed gold glitter . . .

". . . red carpet and velvet ropes, busboys in hot pants, the most fabulous drag queens in Manhattan, and of course we'll need to hire a few actors to masquerade as essential partygoers like Warhol and Grace Jones . . ." Randi went on talking faster and faster as Phyllis nodded her head dizzily, trying to keep up with Randi's barrage of requirements. Sophie didn't need to hear anymore—as far as she was concerned, it was a done deal.

"And, OH!" Phyllis yelled out, causing Sophie to almost jump out of her chair in fright. "I have something to tell you, darling!" Her mother turned to face her and placed a hand on Sophie's arm, squeezing lightly—and this time she didn't dare shrug it off. "The phone call a moment ago? That was the producers from the Pulse Network—your father pulled a few strings, and they want to film the party for a documentary series they're doing on over-the-top sweet sixteens! Isn't that just *perfect?*"

Sophie practically stopped breathing. She'd been watching *My Spoiled Sweet Sixteen* from the second it began airing over two years ago. Being able to have a completely amazing party, *and* be immortalized for future generations to envy was more than she'd ever dreamed of. Sure Madison's sweet sixteen bash at Bungalow 8 had performances by Fergie and the Black Eyed Peas, and featured invitations engraved on the lenses of specially designed pairs of Prada sunglasses, but Sophie's party was going to be legendary, and, to top it all off, not only were there going to be actual celebrities in attendance, she was going to *be* one herself—just like her mom!

"That's amazing!" she cried, jumping to her feet and throwing her arms around her mother before she knew what she was doing. As Phyllis hugged her back, Sophie couldn't help but feel grateful to her mother for knowing exactly what she wanted, even before Sophie knew herself. As she breathed in the scent of her mother's heavy floral perfume, Sophie couldn't help thinking that having two moms might not be so bad after all—even if the one currently hugging her was a liar . . .

To: preynaud@meadowlarkacademy.com
From: aisforapplication@aol.com

Dear Phoebe,

It was a pleasure to meet you yesterday, and I'm looking forward to a busy and productive school year!

I'll be in touch with all of your teachers at Meadowlark, and will instruct them to send me weekly progress reports detailing your class standing and academic progress. I've also requested that your parents send me a complete copy of all your academic transcripts from sixth grade to the present. Unfortunately, your academic achievements before the sixth grade are not kept on file, so if you could supply me with the contact information for your instructors from kindergarten through fifth grade, I'll get in touch with them personally. We're getting a late start—I prefer to begin this process while the student is in the eighth grade—but I intend to more than make up for lost time! As soon as I review this material, I will formulate a program and e-mail you a copy of the game plan. I've also instructed your parents to hire a tutor for your upcoming SAT exam.

Why don't we do breakfast before school next week and discuss this further—say Wednesday at 7 A.M.? I'll call with details and a tentative schedule later this week.

Best,
Andrea

bad
hair
day

Casey sat dejectedly on the front steps of Meadowlark Academy, pulling a strand of her newly shorn hair in between a thumb and forefinger, and stretching it as far as it could possibly go, willing the hair to magically extend past her shoulders. She should've known better than to follow Nanna to the hairdresser yesterday afternoon—from the minute she'd walked in the door of the tiny salon on Eighty-first, Casey knew she was in trouble. Henrietta's Coiffure was filled with more old ladies than a church basement on a Sunday morning, all broiling what was left of their white, silver, or battleship gray hair under long lines of dryers. When Nanna suggested that she get "just the teensiest trim," Casey should've run like her pants were on fire. An hour later her hair was two inches shorter—which wouldn't have been a big deal if she'd been lucky enough to have been born with a *normal* head of hair. But on Casey the cut was an unmitigated disaster—her stupidly curly hair, that she tried every day to tame with a mind-boggling variety of brushes and serums, resisted the scissors violently, and now bounced up past her shoulders in corkscrew curls—in obvious protest of being touched at all. As a result, she now resembled a blond, slightly deranged Carrot Top.

Now, as she glumly sat on the steps outside Meadowlark, surrounded by the bustle of traffic and pedestrians, the blaring of horns, and the sweet toasty scent of roasted nuts wafting through the crisp fall air, all she could think about was what Drew would say when he saw her. Would he run screaming? Start dating Madison again immediately? Put a bag over her head? Casey sighed, wishing she'd worn a hat—or a ski mask. That would definitely solve a myriad of problems . . .

"It's not *that* bad," Sophie said with faux cheerfulness, pushing a curl out of Casey's eyes, clearly lying through her teeth. "Really."

Easy for her to say—Sophie never looked anything but predictably perfect—no matter how crazy her outfit was. For example, today Sophie was wearing an actual *beret*—something that Casey had previously thought only French girls and four-year-olds could get away with. Of course, Sophie's beret was made from super-soft cashmere, and designed by Chanel—along with the tiny, black-and-white tweed skirt she wore, and the matching argyle knee socks. To top it all off, a tight white angora sweater hugged her chest, showing off her B-cups to perfection, and rows of long, creamy white pearls hung around her neck alongside delicate filigree gold chains accented by tinkling charms. On anyone else, it would've looked ridiculous, but Sophie somehow made it work—Frenchified beret and all.

"Don't try and be *nice*, Sophie." Madison giggled, sipping a cup of hot water and lemon she'd bought for lunch, placing the cup down on the cement step and pushing up the sleeves of her ivory sweater dress. "You can't lie about stuff like this—besides, she knows you're lying *anyway*."

Casey nodded. For once, Madison was completely right. She knew she looked like crap—what was the use of pretending?

"Oh, please," Phoebe said with a wave of her hand. "A few weeks in beauty seclusion and she'll be as good as new." Phoebe stabbed the tuna salad she held in her lap with a fork, bringing a bright pink piece of seared tuna to her perfectly outlined crimson lips. Phoebe resembled a pallbearer in her all black ensemble, which included a Peter Som wool jacket and matching skinny-leg wool trousers that ended in black, patent leather Manolo pumps. The bright red glossy lipstick should've made her look like one of the Emo kids that sat at the table in the dining hall farthest away from any windows—in case the weak rays of fall sunlight that streamed through the room somehow marred their scary, pasty flesh. But with her long legs and perfectly proportioned body—not to mention the delicate white-and-rose-gold padlock necklace she wore looped three times around her throat—she looked more like she'd just jumped off the cover of the latest edition of British *Vogue* than someone who moped around their basement whining along with the latest Death Cab for Cutie CD.

"I'm almost afraid to ask what exactly you mean by 'beauty seclusion,'" Casey said dryly, scrunching up the bag of empty potato chips she held in her hand.

"It just means that you don't leave the house for a few weeks," Sophie mumbled, her mouth full of raw carrot sticks. "By the time you resurface, not only has your hair grown out a bit, but everyone's moved on to the latest disaster, and you're in the clear."

"Sounds complicated," Casey said, sighing loudly. "And not very practical—considering I have to go to school."

"Oh my God, *whatever*," Madison snapped, draining the last of her water. "Get your mom to write a note or something. Mine said I had TB last year when that stupid bitch at Fekkai left the developer on my highlights too long, and they turned this totally bilious shade of *green*."

Phoebe and Sophie cracked up, their laughter reverberating in the busy street as Madison glared at them. Sometimes when Phoebe and Sophie laughed like this—at someone else's expense—they reminded Casey of the witches in *Macbeth*: bloodthirsty and vengeful, but with cuter outfits.

"It wasn't *funny*," Mad said, her voice like ice. "It totally ruined the fall quarter—I missed all the good sales and parties, and my hair felt like straw for a *month*."

"*Speaking* of parties," Sophie said breathlessly, snapping the plastic container of raw carrots and celery sticks she held in her lap firmly shut, "you guys are not going to believe what's going on with mine!" Sophie reached into her bag and pulled out a dark blue velvet box with the words H. Stern written on the front in gold lettering, opening the lid to reveal a custom-made white-gold necklace molded into the shape of a letter peeking out of an envelope, minuscule writing looping across the sheet of white gold "paper" in perfect script. Phoebe reached out and grabbed the plush blue box from Sophie's hands, and proceeded to read the tiny text aloud.

"Sophie St. John. The party of the century. The girl of the year. Saturday, October 24th. 9 P.M. Seventies couture requested."

"Are those the *invitations*?" Casey asked, unable to keep the note of total incredulity from her voice. Gold necklaces as sweet sixteen invitations? She was officially not in the Midwest anymore, that was for sure . . .

"I think I'd rather walk down Madison Avenue naked than have to go to another sweet sixteen," Madison said bitchily, raising one blond brow in Sophie's direction.

"Well, you probably shouldn't come then," Sophie said dejectedly. "I guess we'll just have to be on *My Spoiled Sweet Sixteen* without you . . ."

There was a moment of silence as the group took in the atom bomb Sophie had just dropped in Madison's cashmere-covered lap. Casey looked at Madison's astonished expression and felt almost smug. Good for Sophie—she'd succeeded in out-Madisoning Madison for once.

"Are you serious?" Phoebe asked in amazement, a note of excitement creeping into her voice. "We're going to be on Pulse? I can't believe it! What am I going to wear?" she worried aloud, scrunching her brow until horizontal lines appeared in her smooth, pale forehead. "More important," she added, "what are *you* going to wear?"

"Something vintage—definitely," Sophie answered confidently. "We're doing a whole Studio 54 revisited theme—so think Halston, Betsey Johnson, vintage Ralph—anything that screams chic disco seventies."

"That's so cool!" Casey exclaimed, unable to stop herself. "Xanadu is one of my favorite movies of all time!" Casey wondered if showing up in a tube top and roller skates would be out of the question. Now if she could only figure out a way to feather her hair, she'd really be in business . . . Casey woke from her disco lovin' roller skate–wearing fantasy to find the group staring at her uncomprehendingly. "You know," she explained, "it's that movie with Olivia Newton-John where she plays this roller-skating muse? I think it's a Broadway musical now, actually."

"Broadway gives me hives," Madison snapped, obviously miffed at not being the center of attention. "And isn't Xanadu technically eighties anyway?" she said, dismissing Casey's comment with a flick of her wrist like the vision of roller-skating muses itself annoyed her. "Anyway, the Pulse thing is great—it'll be a good way to launch my new modeling career," she added nonchalantly, sliding a pair of Dior aviators over her eyes and staring off into the street.

"*What* modeling career?" Sophie asked uneasily, looking like she was about to regurgitate her carrots at Madison's black-booted feet.

"With Verve Model Management," Madison explained in a bored voice. "It's no big deal—they took some Polaroids and gave me a contract to look over yesterday. I have to show it to Edie this afternoon—she wants to have a 'girls' day' at Elizabeth Arden. I may not survive," she deadpanned, looking over out of the corner of her eyes to gauge Sophie's expression, which was predictably crestfallen. "That reminds me," she said, turning to Casey and pushing her shades on top of her head. "You should come along. My stylist can totally fix *that*." Madison waved one pearly white–varnished nail in the direction of Casey's hair. "And don't worry." Madison grinned like a contented cat. "It's on Edie."

Casey blushed, feeling like a total pauper. She might as well have been standing in the middle of Fifth Avenue with a harmonica and an ugly, flea-infested dog, begging for change. But, no matter how nasty she was, or how she made you feel, Casey knew that it wasn't wise to say no to Madison Macallister—especially when she was offering to do something nice for you. All the same, Casey couldn't help being a little worried about the prospect of Madison becoming a supermodel. If Madison suddenly appeared on the cover of every magazine in Manhattan, would Drew even want to give her the time of day anymore? What would he want with a frizzy-haired mess when he could be dating a world-famous cover girl? *Ugh*, Casey thought, remembering Sophie's party and inwardly groaning. *Just kill me now.* The god-awful haircut she was currently sporting would be immortalized on TV if she didn't take Madison up on her offer, and being dumped for a supermodel was one thing, but having a bad haircut preserved on video for all eternity was something else altogether.

"Thanks," Casey said, watching out of the corner of her eye as Drew exited the front door of Meadowlark and stood on the pavement, squinting into the sunlight. "That would be great." *Please don't let him come over here, please don't let him come over here,* she said silently to herself as Drew turned in their direction, a smile breaking over his face. *Shit,* Casey thought, raising a hand and weakly waving at his approach.

"What's up, ladies?" Drew said with a smile, looking adorable as usual in a pair of brown cords and a military-style khaki jacket. Casey pulled on her hair frantically, praying to anything out there that he wouldn't notice how completely awful she looked.

"We were just discussing Madison's modeling career," Phoebe said proudly, while Madison looked off into the heavily trafficked street as if she couldn't care less.

"What modeling career?" Drew asked, clearly confused by the recent turn of events. Casey watched with something not unlike horror as his blue eyes swept over her face, lingering on her hair, the shock registering on his face like a slap.

"She's signing a contract with Verve," Sophie said woodenly, still stunned at the way she'd been so swiftly dethroned.

"It's so *not* a big deal," Madison said while stifling a yawn, her pink, glossy lips widening as she delicately placed a hand over her mouth. "Excuse me," she said apologetically, "I was up late talking about all this with Antonio—my manager."

"Who's Antonio?" Sophie asked. "Is he Spanish?"

"More important," Phoebe interrupted. "Is he hot?"

"No . . ." Madison said with a slow grin. "And, yes."

"What happened to your *hair?*" Drew blurted out, motioning to Casey's head with one hand and trying like hell to get a word in. Sophie and Phoebe began to giggle, as if on cue, and Casey couldn't help but notice the satisfied expression that moved across Madison's face—an expression that Casey knew would quickly disappear as soon as Drew looked in her direction.

"I got it cut," Casey replied, wishing that the ground—or one of the girls—would simply open up and consume her. Why couldn't there be a trapdoor under your feet, specifically for these kinds of boy-related, completely humiliating moments?

"*Obviously,*" Madison quipped, giggling behind splayed fingers.

"It looks . . ." Drew paused helplessly, trying to find the right words when there were clearly none that could explain how bad she currently looked. ". . . nice," he added weakly, trying to smile.

"It's a hot mess," Madison smirked flirtatiously. "Kind of like you, Drew."

"Whatever." Drew laughed as he rolled his eyes playfully at Mad. "By the way, I wanted to ask you something. I'm making this documentary—well, it's really more of a short film—about rich kids on the UES, and I wanted to see if I could interview you, maybe sometime this week? If you're not too busy with your jet-set lifestyle, that is," Drew added, his voice filled with sarcasm, but his eyes saying something else altogether.

"I'll see if I can fit it in," Madison said airily as she pulled her beeping phone from her Furla tote and scowled at the display.

Casey's stomach turned—the tuna sandwich she'd managed to scarf down in the dining hall before Mad, Pheebs, and Sophie appeared started spinning queasily in her stomach as she watched her kind-of boyfriend stare at his completely gorgeous ex-girlfriend. She felt herself shrinking up and fading into the background as Drew walked away, raising a palm in the air with a halfhearted wave in her direction, before slipping into the front door of Meadowlark, and fading out of sight altogether.

skyrockets
and
flight

Phoebe Reynaud walked along Eighty-third Street, meandering destinationless around the Upper East Side the way she always did when she needed time alone to think. And actually getting some alone time hadn't been exactly difficult today, as Madison and Casey had been scooped up by Edie in her silver Mercedes coupe directly after school let out, and, after a few air kisses in Phoebe's general direction, Sophie had run off for another appointment with her party planner, leaving Phoebe standing on the pavement, antsy, restless, and in no mood to call her dad's car service.

Things with Jared were definitely heating up, and she felt powerless to stop it from happening. After that afternoon in the park, she swore that she was never going to see him again—but later that night when he texted her, she found herself answering back, and the night passed in a flurry of flirtatious, sexy text messages that made her blush just remembering them. Even though it was exciting, Phoebe didn't feel right sneaking around—it made her feel too much like her mother, and right now, there was no one on the planet that she wanted to imitate less than Madeline Reynaud.

As she passed by the window of the new Pinkberry store, she suddenly developed a massive craving for green tea frozen yogurt, and her stomach began to growl softly in the most annoying way possible. Subsisting all day on a few bites of raw tuna was totally exhausting—what she really needed was a small dish of frozen yogurt, with some fresh raspberries on top . . . Five minutes later she was back on the street, cup in hand, her spoon digging into the sweet creamy treat as she walked down the street, the darkness of her mood lifting slightly as the yogurt melted in her mouth, leaving only the acidic, slightly herbal taste of fresh berries and green tea behind.

As she crossed onto Ninety-first Street, Phoebe noticed a familiar figure walking up ahead, her black Jimmy Choo pumps clicking authoritatively on the pavement, a black John Galliano wool cape trimmed in white fox fur swirling around her slim frame. Her head was bent forward, her dark hair pulled back in a twist, a silver cell phone pressed to her ear. Phoebe squinted her eyes, pulling off her sunglasses for a better look, and tossed her half-eaten fro-yo into a metal garbage can at the curb. What was her mother doing down here at this hour? She usually spent every Thursday afternoon at her aerobics class—or so Phoebe had previously thought.

Ever since she'd found those love letters and pictures in

Madeline's closet, Phoebe had avoided her mother as much as humanly possible, spending as much time out of the apartment as she could. Even when she was home, Phoebe preferred to camp out in Bijoux's room rather than have to engage in some forced conversation with her parents—or listen to them fighting, which happened more and more lately. Phoebe's pulse quickened as she realized that Madeline had no idea she was behind her, that this was the perfect opportunity to follow her and find out just who this guy coming so disastrously in between her parents really was.

Madeline's cape swirled around her in a sudden breeze that sent a mass of dried leaves falling to the ground in a rush of orange and brown, and she stopped in front of the Excelsior Grand Hotel, the doorman in his red and gold jacket and cap opening the door for her before she disappeared inside, snapping her cell phone shut in one gloved hand. Phoebe stood at the curb and counted to fifty slowly in her head before approaching the hotel entrance, smiling widely at the doorman as he held open the heavy, ornate door while she slipped inside. The décor of the lobby was strictly Upper East Side chic, which in laymen's terms meant totally boring, with lots of tall, potted palms everywhere, and overstuffed couches and chairs in the lounge area upholstered in creamy shades of bronze and taupe. Phoebe's dark eyes swept the room, searching for the mother's swirling black cape, her heart falling dejectedly as her ears rang with the sound of the elevator doors closing at the far end of the lobby.

Phoebe walked over to the lounge area and sat down on a puffy, beige chair placed strategically behind the green fronds of a potted palm, and slid her sunglasses over her face for good measure. There was no way she could've followed Madeline into the elevator anyway, she told herself. And besides, even if she had somehow managed to trail Madeline to her room without being discovered, she knew that she wouldn't have been able to bring herself to knock on the door. As curious as Phoebe was, she didn't want to confront her mother until she knew more—and certainly not in public. As far as Phoebe knew there was only one way in—or out. Madeline would have to come down sometime. And when she did—preferably with her man in tow—Phoebe would be waiting for her.

Two hours later, Phoebe was totally bored and had exhausted all her entertainment, including her French homework and several rounds of Spot the Prostitute. She closed her French workbook and stretched her arms over her head, yawning loudly as the elevator doors opened with the chiming of bells, and she saw her mother begin to walk through the lobby arm-in-arm with a tall man in jeans and a brown leather jacket, wearing a dark blue fedora that partially obscured his face. Phoebe sank back in her chair and peered through the palm fronds, her heart pounding. Even though the hat blocked most of his face, Phoebe could see enough of it to know for sure that it was the same guy from the picture—for one thing, he had a salt-and-pepper beard.

Phoebe watched awestruck as her mother threw her head back and giggled at something the man whispered in her ear. Phoebe couldn't remember the last time she'd seen her mother laugh at something her father said, and she started to get a hollow feeling in her chest as she watched her mother—obviously so happy—in the arms of another man.

As they approached the front door, the man removed his hat and leaned in for a kiss. As his lips touched Madeline's and they both closed their eyes, Phoebe craned her neck to get a better look, balancing her elbows precariously on the slippery wood of a polished side table. What she saw made her reel back in her chair in shock. The man kissing her mother, making her laugh, meeting her in hotels in the afternoon, sending her love letters, was none other than Drew's father, Robert Van Allen. "Holy shit," Phoebe whispered, clapping a hand over her mouth, suddenly terrified that Madeline would somehow sense her presence and turn around. Luckily for Phoebe, lovers were nothing if not oblivious—and her mother was clearly no exception as she walked out the front door of the hotel with Drew's father, never once giving the lobby, the hotel, or anyone in it, a second glance.

Phoebe sank back in her chair, her thoughts spinning. Not only was she sneaking around behind Sophie's back with Jared, now her mother was sneaking around with Drew's dad, of all people. What were the odds? The Upper East Side had to be the most incestuous zip code on the entire planet! She thought that when she finally found out who her mother was seeing, that she'd somehow magically know what to do next. But as she slung her quilted Chanel tote over her shoulder and stood up, Phoebe Reynaud felt the room tilt dizzily before her eyes. As she walked out the revolving door of the hotel, turning around and around in the circular glass portal, Phoebe knew that it wasn't just the wildly spinning door that was making her feel more turned around than ever before . . .

female
bonding

"Just a bit off the top, darling—I don't want to get scalped," Edie murmured as she stared at her own image reflected in the floor-to-ceiling mirrors that covered the walls of the Elizabeth Arden Red Door Salon. "Bald is *not* a good look for me," she added, patting her chin-length blond bob with one hand.

"Like you would know," Madison snorted from the next chair, her head a mass of silver foils. With the silver tinfoil sticking out of her head, and her slightly smudged eyeliner, Casey realized that this was the only time since she'd met her a month ago that she'd ever seen the teen dream looking less than perfect. It almost made her want to do totally girly things with Mad—like have a sleepover, try on each other's clothes, and let down her guard completely so she could confide all her worries about Drew. *Almost.*

"Darling," Edie continued, totally oblivious to Madison's sarcasm, "strange things happened in the seventies, you know. And I was there," she said dreamily as the black-clad stylist standing behind her began to separate her hair into sections with the pointy end of a steel comb. "We all were," she added, raising a glass of white wine to her lips and draining it in one thirsty gulp.

O . . . kay . . . Casey thought, catching Madison's eye in the mirror. Madison rolled her eyes and shot Casey a "what the fuck" expression that was so totally what Casey had been thinking that they both cracked up at the same time, shoulders shaking.

"Stop moving," Madison's stylist hissed as she affixed the last piece of silver foil in place with a hard pat to Mad's platinum blond head. "Do you want your highlights to be crooked?"

"Well, I don't know," Madison asked sweetly. "Do you want to get paid?" The stylist, her own hair twisted into a blond French twist, gave Madison a hard, tight smile to match her hairdo. Madison simply ignored her, sipping slowly at her own glass of white wine and inspecting her face in the mirror.

"God, I look like a wreck," she moaned, swiping at the smudged liner with two long fingers. "I am so not ready for this test shoot tomorrow."

"Tomorrow?" Casey asked with surprise. Wow—when fame beckoned, it certainly moved at the speed of light. Casey couldn't help but wonder what it would feel like to have people that excited about her—and as much as she hated it, she couldn't help feeling a little jealous of Madison's endless good fortune. Why

did amazing things always happen to people who already had everything they could ever want or need? "Don't you have to talk to Edie first?"

"Technically"—Madison sighed—"I need to show her the contract and get her permission and all that." Madison frowned into the mirror, clearly finding the prospect of doing so less than thrilling. "I'll just do it later on after she's had her tenth drink and fourth Valium of the day," she said bitterly, looking down at her lap, which was covered by a silver vinyl cape.

It was at times like these that Casey caught glimpses of exactly who the girl behind the perfect Upper East Side veneer really was—and as much as Madison wanted people to believe that she had it all, Casey knew that in reality, Madison was strangely, inexplicably sad, and very lonely. At moments like these, Casey wanted more than ever to become Madison's real friend—when she was vulnerable, when her guard was let down even for just a second, Casey caught a glimpse of the real person behind Madison's carefully constructed façade and wanted, more than anything, to know her. Casey snapped out of her thoughts as French twist girl came up behind her, holding strands of Casey's unruly blond curls between her fingers.

"Now, what are we going to do with *you*?" she inquired coolly, looking at Casey's hair like it was infested with bugs. "Do you *like* your hair this curly?"

"Uh, *no*," Casey deadpanned, looking at the stylist like she'd gone completely insane. "But it's not like I've really got a choice."

"I can chemically straighten it for you if you want," the stylist said offhandedly as she attempted to get a metal comb through a mass of snarls in the back of Casey's head, giving up after a few seconds and throwing the comb on her station exasperatedly. "Should last anywhere from four to six months."

Casey's mouth fell open as she stared at the stylist uncomprehendingly. Chemical straightening? Why had she never heard of this? "Let me get this straight," she started slowly, "you can give me straight hair? Like straight straight? Straight like *hers*?" she finished, pointing at Madison who was giggling softly from behind the latest issue of *In Touch*.

"Well, not *exactly* like hers," the stylist answered, "I mean it won't be platinum, but, yeah, I can straighten it—if that's what you *want*."

"Yes!" Casey shouted a little too loudly, her face turning red as most of the salon turned around to stare at her. "That's what I want," she added more quietly, turning to Madison. "Did you know they could do this?"

"Duh," Mad said, engrossed in a story about Posh and Becks keeping separate bedrooms. "Everybody knows about straightening—how do you think Phoebe's hair looks so good?" she added triumphantly. "But, truthfully, her hair is really more wavy than curly—she just likes to have it ultra-smooth. She doesn't do it very often—but you certainly will. *Your* hair is like corkscrew central," she said with a smile, turning the glossy page, the huge emerald ring on her left hand sparkling in the light.

"But not for long," Casey whispered under her breath as the stylist left to mix up the straightening solution. She couldn't quite believe it: She was finally going to have the one thing she'd wanted more than anything for her entire life, the thing she thought was totally unattainable—completely straight hair. And when Drew saw her, hopefully she'd look so amazing that he'd forget all about Madison and her glamorous career. There was nothing like a makeover to make a boy pay strict attention, and Casey planned on looking so good that Drew wouldn't be able to take his eyes off of her—not even for a second . . .

model
behavior

"That's it, love. Cock your hip for me and give me those killer eyes . . ."

Sam Wise flew around the huge loft with the grace of a crazed jackrabbit as he leaped and jumped before the dazed-looking model posed before a glaring white backdrop, her straw-colored hair falling over one eye, her hand on her hip as she stared into the lens with an expression that suggested that she'd rather be home cutting her cuticles than standing in front of the camera swathed in designer loot. The model was a walking exercise in jadedness—as far as Madison could tell, she'd spent the majority of the shoot so far trying to look as bored as possible as the flash exploded in her face, giving her the expression of a startled deer.

Madison threw her trench over her shoulder, arms crossed

over her black cashmere sweater, her jeans stuffed into knee-high black crocodile Manolo boots. She was still traumatized from the ridiculously long car ride to Williamsburg. She shivered, drawing her coat closer to her, hoping to ward off the obviously contagious bad fashion plague that haunted the neighborhood—so many boys couldn't possibly be wearing such tight jeans by *choice*. And going anywhere in Brooklyn just wasn't natural in the first place—the subway went underwater for God's sake! Not that she'd know from personal experience, of course—she'd rather die than take the train . . .

As she watched the model stretch out on the floor, her chin raised to the lens, she was decidedly unimpressed. Madison knew somehow instinctively that, as nervous as she was about getting in front of the camera, there was no doubt that she could pose way better than some emaciated fish stick with no tits and zero sex appeal. The girl threw her hair back over her shoulders, and thrust her nonexistent breasts out for the camera. This was all the more comical considering that she was wearing a giant blue ball gown—quite possibly one of the unsexiest outfits on the planet. *She looks like she got lost on the way to prom,* Madison snickered silently as she looked around, taking in the brilliant white walls and the endless hustle of photographers' assistants milling around the room holding expensive-looking cameras in their hands. The assistants were all dressed so similarly that it looked as though they were in uniform—the same tight black jeans and dirt-colored hoodies up top, the same high-concept dark eyeglasses, the same choppy haircuts. Madison could tell she was in Williamsburg just by looking at them.

"All right—where's my next victim?" a voice called out, the

words reverberating over the annoying, incessant house music booming through the room. Sam Wise walked over to Madison, sizing her up on the short journey over, his appreciative gaze sweeping from the roots of her hair to her booted feet in a matter of seconds. Sam Wise was in his mid-to-late forties, with dark, gray-streaked hair and a matching beard atop a totally worked-out bod—which was highlighted to perfection by the cutoff sleeves of his Strokes T-shirt and tight, ripped, faded jeans. Despite the body, he wasn't quite the hotness—there was something about his face that was a little *too* angular, his body a little *too* ripped to be genuinely gorgeous. And his thick British accent made it sound like he had about a pound of marbles rolling around in his mouth . . .

"I'm Madison Macallister," Madison said in her most businesslike voice as she stuck out her hand for Sam to shake. Sam just stood there looking at her hand in front of his like it was a dead fish—or a plus-sized model—and shot her a nasty grin as he took drags off a truly foul-smelling clove cigarette with one hand, rubbing his unmanicured beard with the other. "I'm here for my test shoot?"

"Sure you are, love," Sam said lazily, pointing with his gross cigarette to the back of the loft. "Trot on back there and put on the swimsuit in the dressing room."

Oh. No. He. Didn't. A swimsuit? Hello? She thought this was a high-fashion shoot—not a *Maxim* cover. And *trot*? Did she look like she was wearing a fucking bridle?

"Swimsuit?" Madison said weakly, dropping her hand to her side. "Antonio didn't tell me I'd be wearing a bathing suit today."

"*I'm* telling you," Sam shot back, on the verge of nastiness.

"Now trot on back, love, before I lose what's left of my patience." And, with that, Sam turned his back on her sharply and began arguing with an assistant sporting an actual mullet—he probably thought it was ironic—and an Elliott Smith T-shirt, in a heated tone of voice.

Madison took a deep breath and exhaled loudly, wishing she'd taken one of Edie's Valiums before she left the apartment this morning—she could definitely stand for being a little more relaxed right now—especially since she was about to get almost-naked in front of a sleazy photographer and half the hipster population of Williamsburg. As she pulled back the curtain to the dressing room, Madison gazed at the swimsuit hanging up on the wall in horror. She picked it up like it was a tarantula, turning it over in her hands in disbelief. Okay, it was Dior, but the actual bathing suit consisted of little more than a few strands of black dental floss that were meant to crisscross her body, barely covering her naughty bits. In the not-helping-things-department, the back of the suit was the most hated of all bathing suit designs—a thong. Basically, there was going to be one narrow strip of dental floss up her ass, effectively exposing all the lumps and bumps on her behind in the most unflattering way possible.

It was official—she was doomed.

Well, there was nothing to be done about it. *Unless I manage to cut off my circulation with all these strings and drop dead,* Madison thought as she stepped out of her boots and jeans, her hands like ice. As she was struggling to tie the suit in such a way that it covered most of her unmentionables, she heard a gruff voice outside the cubicle.

"You all right in there, love? You need any help getting into that thing?"

Madison grabbed her boobs with one hand, and peered out of the curtain at Sam's lecherous face, wishing she had a stun gun or a cattle prod. Why did old guys have to be such dirty old men?

"No," she said firmly, making sure the curtain covered ever inch of her, "I'm fine. I'll be out in a minute." She snapped the curtain shut with all the dignity she could muster, not relaxing until she heard the sound of his boots on the cement floor walking away from the dressing room. She wished more than anything that there was a mirror in the dressing room so she could check and make sure every bit she could actually cover was hidden—but no such luck. *Makes sense—if the models actually saw what they were wearing, there's no way they'd ever leave this room.* Madison giggled softly to herself out of nervousness more than anything else, and threw back the curtain with a deep breath. So the photographer was a sleaze—who cared? It wasn't exactly the first time some random guy had tried to get into her pants. She bent down and held her head upside down, then stood up quickly, flipping her hair back so that it had some fullness, and walked, barefoot, out into the center of the studio toward Sam, who was scowling at one of his cameras. The bustle of the room stopped completely as she stood there, and Madison suddenly became acutely aware that every pair of eyes in the room was focused on her. She crossed her arms over her chest, and bit her bottom lip, wishing she could disappear. She'd never felt so . . . exposed in her life.

"That looks smashing, love," Sam said appreciatively, with a little too much enthusiasm for Madison's taste. "Trot over to the backdrop and stand on the X on the floor, all right?" Sam placed one hand on Madison's shoulder, his fingers massaging her flesh as he led her over to a small red X painted on the floor. Madison stood there awkwardly, the lights in her face blinding her completely. She felt like she could barely keep her eyes open—the lights were practically shrieking they were so fucking bright. She felt so totally naked—didn't models usually get their hair done or at the very least couldn't they spackle some more makeup on her face?

"Don't I need makeup?" she asked tentatively, bringing a hand up to her cheek as Sam raised the camera to his face.

"You look perfect, darling. Just perfect." As Sam stared at her through the lens, his tongue wagged out of the corner of his mouth, wetting his thin lips lasciviously. "Now, give me some attitude—one hand on your hip. Yes, that's lovely . . ."

As she stood there trying not to squint into the light, a hand on her hip, Madison had the most curious sensation of being shrunk down to fit into the camera lens, her image trapped and preserved there in a slick dark image that hundreds of eyes would peruse. It made her feel slightly sweaty and queasy, and she hoped to God that she wouldn't start perspiring like a linebacker standing there, trying her best to ooze sex appeal when she felt about as attractive as a dead fish. And *trying* to be sexy never worked—she just looked like a dork when she forced it. It wasn't like she could really relax when Sam was looking at her like she was wearing his lunch. As the camera flashed around her relentlessly, she knew deep in her soul that she looked stupid and awkward and, most of all, stiff as a board.

The problem was, so did the photographer.

"All right, that's enough," Sam said with annoyance, lowering the camera and scowling at her. "Are you sure you're cut out for this, love?" Sam asked as he popped another cigarette into his mouth, one of his assistants running over to light the tip. Madison nodded, unable to speak. At that moment, she didn't even really care if she'd blown it—all she wanted was to get her clothes back on and get the hell out of there. Without uttering another word she dropped her eyes to the floor and practically ran to the back of the studio, pulling the dressing room curtains roughly closed.

Once inside, the disappointment washed over her like a tidal wave, and she held onto the wall, willing herself not to cry. So, she'd blown it. There'd be other chances—there had to be. After all, she was Madison Macallister! And that had to mean *something*, didn't it? Bending over, she struggled back into her tight jeans, shoving her feet into her socks and boots, worrying that if she stopped for a moment, she might lose it. Just as she was about to pull her sweater over her head, she felt a rush of cold air on her back, and a hand on her shoulder. She yelled out, whirling around to face Sam, who stood there with a peculiar look on his face.

"Shhhhhh, babe. No yelling," he said with a wry smile, reaching up and smoothing her hair from her face with one large, meaty hand. "We don't want everyone coming in here, now do we?"

Madison watched as if in a trance, as Sam's hand slipped from her face to her shoulder, then made its way down toward her naked breast. What the fuck? Was there a giant sign on her forehead that read AMERICA'S NEXT TOP PROSTITUTE? *Don't panic*, she told herself. *Just don't fucking panic.* And then—before she could think to scream or call out—her body took over as she brought one denim-clad knee up between his legs, knocking him senseless.

"You little bitch." Sam groaned, staggering out of the curtain to the amused faces of his team, and falling onto the hard cement floor, his hand between his legs, his face contorted in pain.

"Oh yeah?" Madison retorted, shoving her head into her sweater and throwing her trench over her shoulders, then placing both hands on her hips defiantly. "Well, it's better to be *called* a little bitch than to *act* like one—don't you think?"

Madison jumped as the studio erupted in applause and the hipster entourage clapped for her en masse as she walked across the floor purposefully, praying Sam wouldn't suddenly regain his strength and follow her before she made it to the exit. As she slammed the door behind her, still shaking, Madison's tough-girl veneer fell away, and the tears that had come so close to falling in the dressing room now stained her cheeks as she stepped into the large freight elevator, pulling the door closed behind her.

girls
on
film

Being in the same, small space with an ex and a current crush was always a less than desirable situation—and one Drew was now experiencing firsthand. The prospect of trying to film a documentary with his ex as an interviewee and his crush as his helper was proving to be nothing less than a nightmare. It was an afternoon that Drew had been dreading—and one he could've kicked himself for setting up in the first place. He knew, even as the words left his lips, that including Madison in the movie was a bad idea on *so* many levels—but as he stood there yesterday afternoon listening to her talk about her burgeoning modeling career, the sun slicing through her platinum hair, he just couldn't seem to stop himself. And when she mentioned that Antonio guy, his blood really started to boil for reasons he couldn't quite explain to anyone in the immediate vicinity—much less himself.

"Could you move that light over just a bit," Drew asked Casey as he peered through the lens of his camera where Madison's perfect—albeit badly lit—visage filled the frame. Casey began to move the lamp in question and in the viewfinder Drew could see the hard shadow cutting underneath Madison's nose float away and soften, dispersing over the perfect angles of her cheek. "*There*," Drew said. "Don't move it an inch, Casey—she looks perfect—and you're not so bad yourself," he added with a smile, taking in Casey's new 'do, the silkily straight golden hair that now fell to her shoulders and shone under the hot lights. Casey immediately blushed in that way Drew absolutely loved, bringing one hand up to her neck and raking it through her newly straightened hair, a look of wonder on her face—as though she couldn't quite believe those soft strands running through her fingers so effortlessly were her own. Truth be told, Casey's new hair definitely looked hot, but, all hotness aside, he kind of missed her untamable tumble of curls. With her new, straight hair Casey looked undeniably gorgeous, but kind of ordinary. Without her curls, and wearing a black sweater and yellow and green plaid mini that looked suspiciously like it had been plucked from Mad's overstuffed closet, Casey looked almost like every other Upper East Side princess he saw on a daily basis. And, at the end of the day, Drew wasn't sure how much he really dug Casey's new look. Wasn't he dating her because she was so *different* than the other girls at Meadowlark? *It's just hair*, he told himself, wiping his moist brow with one hand. *Stop being such a woman about everything . . .*

"It's a vast improvement—brought about by yours truly, of course," Madison said jokingly, pointing at her chest, which was covered by a satiny beige blouse that tied at the neck in a huge, expertly tied bow, the full sleeves spotlighting her long, delicate hands. Throwing back her blond tresses over her shoulders, she stared into the curving, black eye of the camera, her gaze cutting through all of the exactingly cut glass and the maze of complex hardware into Drew's own eye, the intensity and beauty of the deep green hue making something curl up and flip over deep inside his stomach.

Is she coming on to me? Drew thought, a nervous sweat breaking out on his palms. Being in the same room with Mad and Casey would be difficult if Mad was in a *coma*. If she was going to turn it all on like she seemed to be doing, it was going to be impossible—impossible for his head, heart, and pants to make it through this day intact. Drew shot a quick glance at Casey to see if she'd noticed Mad's smoldering look—or his admittedly sweaty response—but she was bent over, fiddling with a snaky pile of white extension cords, and hadn't seen a thing, or at least that's what he told himself . . .

"So we're almost ready then, right, Drew?" Casey said, straightening up, her eyes scanning the production checklist that she held on a clipboard in one hand, the other tweaking the knobs of the sound deck. "The lighting is set. The sound is set. We can go ahead and shoot."

"Oh," Madison said, her eyes breaking away from the camera, that unearthly halogenlike glow she had been radiating, catching

Drew so incredibly off guard, dimming down to her regular, eighty-watt output, "I thought we were already filming."

Drew looked up from the viewfinder and again caught Madison's gaze. The spark, the smolder, the sex that had been there just seconds before was almost completely gone and she quickly looked away, a wandering hand reaching up to twirl a strand of hair around her finger. *It's the camera*, Drew realized. *She couldn't care* less *about me—it's all for the camera. She lights up, comes alive in front of it.* There was no doubt about it—Madison Macallister was a star.

"Okay," Drew said, trying to sound as businesslike as possible as he pressed record and the red light atop the camera began to blink. "We're rolling." Drew pulled away from the camera and consulted the set of questions he'd printed out hours before, holding the piece of white computer paper in front of him like a shield.

"So, what's it like being rich?" he asked bluntly, trying to get the ball rolling as Mad stared at him unblinkingly, her face glowing like a fallen star in the harsh white light of the halogen bulbs.

"You tell me," Madison said evenly, a half-smile turning up the corners of her lips.

"Very funny," Drew said sarcastically. His dark hair flopped down over his eyes, and he pushed it back with annoyance before continuing. "What does being rich mean to *you?*"

"Well," Mad said, looking thoughtful, "the politically correct answer would probably be that I don't have to wait in line, I have endless options, and get whatever I want—at the expense of everyone else."

Drew's mouth fell open slightly. Jesus—in the relatively short time they'd known each other it was probably the most thoughtful answer Madison had ever given him about anything even *remotely* political. Who was this poised, thoughtful, gorgeous girl sitting in front of him? As he watched her ready herself for the next onslaught of questioning, Drew was filled with the sneaking suspicion that he might not know Madison as well as he thought he did . . .

"But it's all I've ever really known, so it's kind of hard to be objective about it," Madison continued, her gaze level, her voice calm and purposeful. "It's probably a hard question for you to ask—and a tougher one for me to answer."

"Well, give it a shot," Drew said with a grin.

"Talking about money is vulgar," Madison said with obvious distaste. "I feel all itchy just thinking about it." Drew watched as Mad proceeded to rub her slim arms through the slippery satin of her blouse.

"When was the first time you realized you were rich?" Drew asked, changing the subject and attacking the topic from another angle.

"Hmmmm . . ." Madison cocked her head to the side, looking thoughtfully into the lens again, her green eyes catching the light. "I think I was around six, and we had this Guatemalan housekeeper who used to bring her little girl to work with her—she was about my age." Madison reached over to Drew's desk and grabbed a bottle of Evian, taking a long swallow before continuing. "Anyway, she was always totally amazed by all my toys and stuff, and that's when I realized that not everyone lived the way I did."

Drew glanced over at Casey, who was seated on the edge of his bed, the yellow and green plaid skirt she wore clashing spectacularly with his blue and orange Ralph Lauren plaid comforter. She was watching Madison attentively, a rapt expression on her freckled face.

"Does being wealthy influence what you plan to do with your life?" Drew asked, leaning into the camera and checking to make sure the shot was still perfect. "How does modeling fit in?"

"Well, obviously I don't *have* to work or anything." Madison gave the camera a tight smile. "But knowing I have money means it's not such a big deal if I end up sucking at it."

"Why not?" Drew asked, genuinely curious. "I'd think there'd be even *more* pressure on you to succeed at modeling since everyone knows you're wealthy—don't you worry about people saying that the only reason anyone even pays attention to you is because of your parents' money?"

"If I worried about what people said all the time I'd be in a locked psych ward," Madison snapped, "not on the verge of signing a major modeling contract."

"You haven't signed it yet?" Casey asked with amazement, pulling her legs beneath her on the bed until she was sitting cross-legged. "I thought you were going to talk to Edie yesterday?"

"I was," Madison said with annoyance, brushing a pale piece of hair from her face. "I *am*. I just haven't gotten around to it yet."

"Speaking of your mom," Drew interrupted, "did finances have anything to do with your parents' decision to split up last year?"

Madison opened her mouth, then closed it again, speechless. She stared into the lens, her confident and slightly irritated expression crumpling like a white, unlined sheet of paper in Drew's fist. "It wasn't . . ." she sputtered. "It didn't . . ." Her mouth began to turn down at the corners, and she suddenly turned her face away from the camera for the first time, her face glowing in profile, one tear sliding down her cheek as she cried without sound, her shoulders shaking. "They couldn't," she continued, her voice breaking, "they just didn't . . . love each other . . . anymore."

"Shit," Drew muttered under his breath, getting up and grabbing a box of Kleenex off his night table and handing it to Madison, who grabbed a tissue and dabbed her eyes carefully so as not to smear the navy liner on her top lids. Drew knelt down at her feet, placing one hand on her knee. Even if she wasn't his girlfriend anymore, he still hated to see her cry, and most of all he hated the idea that it was his stupid, thoughtless question that had *made* her cry in the first place.

"Hey, Mad," he said quietly, forgetting the camera still humming quietly, the red light blinking, and the fact that his new girlfriend was in the room, her eyes following his every move. "I'm sorry." She looked over at him, the tears still making their way slowly down her face, muting the color of her electric green eyes, and placed her hand on top of his, the warmth of her skin like an electric shock shooting through his body. What was going on with him lately? Just when he thought he was ready to make Madison a part of his past forever, moments like this made it clear that shoving Mad to the back of the line of his life wasn't going to be as simple as he'd originally thought.

"It's all right," she said, pulling her hand away and blowing her red nose. "We can finish."

"You sure?" Drew asked, standing up and running a hand through his hair. "It's just a stupid documentary."

"It's *not* stupid," Casey said from her post on the bed, maybe a little too sharply. Casey stared down at her knees, biting her bottom lip and kicking one black ballet slipper against the other before getting up and walking quickly to the door, her hair swinging like a flag from the rush of air as she closed it firmly behind her.

"What's up with *her*?" Mad asked, throwing her used tissue to the floor and crossing one slim leg over the other.

Drew shrugged, taking a seat behind the camera again and rechecking the shot. He knew that he should probably go after Casey—that's what a good boyfriend would do. Drew knew that when girls left a room like that—obviously upset—they generally wanted you to follow them. But as strong as the feeling in his gut was that told him to get moving *pronto*, his feet were somehow cemented to the thick, navy carpeting of his room.

"So," Mad said, her teeth shining like a string of polished pearls under the lights, her composure regained. "Fire away."

As Drew looked down at his sheet of questions, and then the empty space on the bed where Casey had sat moments before, the empty space grew larger and larger until it filled both the room—and his brain. He knew, from the sinking feeling in his stomach, that, by continuing to sit here with Madison, he might've just blown things with Casey for good.

secrets
and
lies

"Are you sure you don't want anything to eat with that?"
Jared pointed at the mug of chamomile tea resting on the table,
the steam rising from the chipped blue cup and obscuring
Phoebe's face. Phoebe shook her head, wrapping her cold fingers around the hot cup, grateful for the cloud of steam that
hung between them like a curtain. Maybe if she just kept ordering tea, the white, gauzy steam would completely hide the fact
that she couldn't look Jared in the face without imagining his
lips on hers, the sweet, forbidden pressure of his mouth, and
the way his eyes misted over when they finally pulled away from
one another.

Phoebe forced herself to look away from his sharply chiseled
face, and at the horrendous "art" adorning the walls that looked

as though it was fashioned from yards of red string and copious white puka shells. The Potted Fern was a macramé disaster on Ninety-sixth Street and Park, decorated with gross hippie art and overflowing with plants, green tendrils hanging down from the watermarked ceiling, tickling the shoulders and faces of unsuspecting diners. Since the place was the total polar opposite of anything even remotely *approaching* cool, Phoebe knew there was zero chance that she'd run into anyone she knew there. Still, she couldn't help looking around nervously every few minutes as the door swung open . . .

"So, what's going on?" Jared said, dumping half the sugar container into his black coffee and stirring the dark liquid slowly, his eyes locked on hers. "You sounded pretty upset on the phone." Just watching his long hands stirring his coffee, she wanted more than anything to be the spoon, to be slid sensuously between those full red lips . . . *Get it together*, she told herself, dropping her gaze to the chipped Formica tabletop. *You are such a sex beast lately* . . . And the brown leather jacket he wore with a dark blue Billabong T-shirt—slightly ripped at the neck—sent the smell of tanned leather across the table in waves, mixing with his signature scent of ripe citrus and salt that made her want to pass out—just so he could press his lips to hers and resuscitate her.

"I was walking home yesterday, and I saw my mom go into a hotel."

Jared halted his cup in midair on the path to his lips. "Uh-oh," he said, his blue eyes narrowing cynically. "Let me guess—she wasn't exactly meeting your dad, right?"

"You got it." Phoebe exhaled loudly, pushing the cup away and leaning her elbows on the table. "But that's not the worst part."

"It gets worse?" Jared smirked, raising an eyebrow.

"Definitely." Phoebe said, poking one finger through a hole in the sleeves of her pale blue sweater. She'd purposefully worn her grossest clothes today and not washed her hair this morning—just to prove to herself that she definitely wasn't interested in him. Why spend hours picking out the perfect outfit when she was *so* not dating him anyway? "Jared, you can't tell anyone what I'm about to tell you," Phoebe began, her voice solemn and slow.

"Why tell *me?*" Jared asked, draining the last of his coffee and pushing the cup to the side. "Why not tell my sister—or one of your other little friends?"

Now it was Phoebe's turn to smirk across the table. "As much as I love your sister, you and I both know that she wouldn't be able to keep her mouth shut about this—and I know you will."

"How do you know?" Jared whispered, reaching across the table and taking her hand in his, folding her fingers into his own.

"Because I'm asking you to," Phoebe answered, aware that she was barely breathing as his grip tightened. With considerable effort, Phoebe forced herself to pull away, putting both of her hands under the table—and out of his reach.

"All right," Jared said, nodding slowly while simultaneously shrugging his arms out of his leather jacket. At the sight of his caramel-colored, slightly muscled biceps, Phoebe felt like she was about to fall into a swoon. Wait—didn't that only happen to maidens in nineteenth-century novels whose corsets were pulled too tight? What excuse did she have for feeling so dizzy and strange at the sight of Jared's bare flesh?

"Well, I waited for my mom to come down from the room and leave the hotel—it took forever. And when she finally showed up she wasn't exactly alone, if you know what I mean." Phoebe paused, cracking her knuckles nervously under the table the way she always did when she was worried or nervous—or both. "She was with Drew's *dad*," Phoebe finished, the words coming out in a rush.

"You're kidding me." Jared raised a hand and motioned to the waitress for a refill. "Weird. The Van Allens always seemed so happy to me," Jared mused aloud as the waitress refilled his cup, the rich, dark aroma of roasted coffee beans perfuming the air.

"I know," Phoebe agreed, pulling her own cup of lukewarm tea toward her and sipping the tepid, floral-scented liquid. "That's why it's so strange. I mean, was it an *act* all this time? I always thought they were the happiest couple on the Upper East Side."

"Yeah, me too." Jared raised the cup to his lips, then put it back down, wiping his mouth on a paper napkin before continuing. "Maybe it wasn't an act, Phoebe—maybe things just *change*."

"I guess," Phoebe said morosely, more depressed than ever. "I mean, I look at my own parents and I *know* that they must've been happy once, right?" Phoebe took a deep breath and went on before Jared could begin to speak. She felt like if she didn't keep talking, she'd probably just explode all over the macramé wall hangings, making the hideous décor even uglier. "They must've been in love at some point—and if they were then where did that love *go*?" Phoebe dropped her head to the table, resting it on her forearms. "Ugh. I sound like a bad pop song," she said with a moan.

Jared laughed, reaching across the table and placing his hand on her arm. At the touch of his warm skin on hers Phoebe sat up as if she'd been scalded by a cup of hot water, pulling her arm away from him for the second time. Phoebe looked out the window at the passersby: a woman in a ranch mink jacket strolled by, a dachshund puppy wearing a Burberry sweater tucked beneath one arm. Steam swirled out of the sewer grates at the curb and into the rapidly darkening gray October sky. For reasons she couldn't explain to Jared, and certainly not to herself, she felt her eyes beginning to well up with tears. Why couldn't she just have a normal family—one that ate dinner together every night and actually asked each other questions about their day? Why couldn't she have a family that really loved each other in a way that was both true and permanent? Phoebe knew down deep in her heart that she'd trade it all—the luxury apartment, the money, her endless collection of bags and shoes—for a family life that didn't make her want to cry every day, for parents who still loved each other. Every time she walked through the front door of her apartment, it was like walking into prison. The tension in the air was so incredibly thick that she tiptoed around on eggshells, never sure when her parents would begin fighting again. The death knell of their soured relationship hung solidly in the air like thunder before a heavy rainstorm—and it filled the apartment and her life with the most horrible sense of expectation. It wasn't that Phoebe necessarily *wanted* her parents to get divorced, but she wasn't sure how much longer she and Bijoux could keep living this way. As much as she hated the idea of her family splitting up, sometimes the thought of being able to live without the constant fighting didn't sound like such a bad idea . . .

"It just makes me wonder," Phoebe went on, blinking back the tears, her eyelashes slapping against the skin of her cheeks, her arm still tingling from where he'd touched her, "can *anyone* live happily ever after anymore without cheating?" She looked up, her eyes meeting Jared's level gaze, and held her breath, goose bumps popping up all over her body.

"I think I could," Jared said softly, his blue eyes never leaving hers. "With someone like you."

Phoebe's mouth fell slightly open, and she closed it in a hurry, trying to hide the shocked expression that must've been all over her face. Jared reached across the table determinedly, taking her hand in his own again, and holding on firmly, his fingers sliding down to wrap around her bare wrist.

"Meet me tomorrow night at midnight in the entertainment lounge," he whispered, his eyes locking on hers with an intensity that scared and thrilled her all at once. She felt hypnotized as she nodded wordlessly, watching in slow motion as he pulled her to him across the table. Before Phoebe knew what she was doing, she was on her feet and leaning forward, her lips touching his with a shock of surprising softness—right in the middle of a hideous coffee shop on Ninety-sixth and Park. As she closed her eyes and finally surrendered, she didn't care who saw them together, stretched across the red vinyl booth—she was lost in the warmth of his kiss and the strength of the hand that held her captive. And, captive or not, all Phoebe knew was that she never wanted to get away—even if it made her feel uncomfortably close to becoming her own cheating, philandering mother, even if it meant sneaking around for the whole rest of her life.

Even if it meant betraying her best friend.

grandmotherly advice

"Casey Anne, I know it's been a bad day when I see you digging into the ice cream *right* after dinner," Nanna cackled, as she loaded their dinner dishes into the dishwasher, and switched it on with a loud rumble that filled the room with ambient noise.

Casey sighed, looking around Nanna's comfortable gray and white kitchen, at the white rag rug on the floor, the gray linoleum, and the chipped white kitchen cabinets with their tarnished brass knobs. Nanna's kitchen definitely wasn't as luxurious as the lavish restaurant-style spaces that most of the residents of The Bramford installed, but, then again, Nanna wasn't exactly rich either. The first time Casey had remarked on the difference between Nanna's kitchen and Sophie's, Nanna had emitted a loud snort. "Those are kitchens wasted on people who don't even know how to cook! Fancy marble countertops and hulking stainless steel refrigerators—for what? So they can order take-out every night, *that's* what!" Nanna yelled triumphantly, smacking her hand down on her own granite countertop for added emphasis.

Nanna and Casey's grandfather had gotten into The Bram back when it was relatively reasonable—and the fact that their apartment was quickly rent stabilized didn't hurt either . . . When Casey's grandfather passed away a few years ago, Nanna had decided to stay on. "New York is my life," she was fond of stating defiantly. "And The Bram is my home—you'll have to drag me out of here in a box." So far, anyway, Casey's family knew better than to even try.

"It wasn't a *bad* day exactly," Casey said, digging a spoon into a rock-hard pint of Ben and Jerry's Cherry Garcia. She hated cherries, but right now she'd probably eat her own arm if it were smothered in chocolate. "More like an unqualified disaster."

Nanna halted wiping the kitchen counter with a sponge to shoot Casey an annoyed look. "You sound like the spitting image of your mother with all that fancy-pants talk!"

Casey's mother, Barbara McCloy, was a professor of Women's Studies back at Illinois State, who was currently on sabbatical for a year, probably at this moment flitting around London and pretending to be an academic. From what Casey could tell, Barbara spent all her time at fancy teahouses and pubs—and a limited amount of time in the library, where she was *supposed* to be researching a book on the history of women and gossip to be published sometime next year by Seal Press. As her mother was a militant feminist who rarely bought new clothes and instead gave Casey endless amounts of grief about hers, the last thing she wanted was to remind anyone of Barbara . . .

"Since I haven't talked to my mother in weeks, it's probably the fancy-pants school I'm attending," Casey said dejectedly, scraping a thin layer of ice cream off the top of the container and sliding the spoon into her mouth. "Soon I won't even sound like a normal person."

"Casey, honey," Nanna said, turning around, the choker-length strand of pearls she always wore matching the luster of her silver hair perfectly. "I hate to break it to you, but you never really *did*."

"I know." Casey moaned, her mouth full of rapidly melting ice cream. "Thanks for pointing that out, Nanna."

Nanna sat down at the kitchen table, running her hand over the bleached pine surface that was nicked and scarred from years of use, and took her gold bifocals from a pearl chain around her neck and slid them over her nose. Nanna didn't ever believe in "comfortable" clothes or in dressing down, which explained her perfectly pressed wool trousers and white cashmere turtleneck. As always, a beloved pair of black Chanel ballet flats adorned her tiny feet. *Those flats are probably older than I am*, Casey thought with a smile. Although Nanna could often be a royal pain in the ass—especially when she refused to wear her hearing aid—she was, far and away, Casey's favorite family member. Not that it was a difficult honor to obtain or anything, considering that her mom called once every two weeks—if that—from London, and her dad, having recently been fired from a dotcom in Seattle, called even less frequently. And even when he did manage to pick up the phone, their conversations had lately been reduced to such scintillating topics as the weather, and the state of New York post-Giuliani.

Casey stuck her spoon into the ice cream, moved over to the kitchen table, and sat down beside Nanna, placing the container between them and offering Nanna the spoon.

"So, what's going on in the glamorous world of Upper East Side infighting?" Nanna asked, a smirk lighting up her soft, deeply lined face. "And what's happened to your *hair*?" Nanna asked, melodramatic horror animating her voice as she reached out and smoothed a strand of Casey's already-smooth locks.

"Madison took me to get it straightened," Casey said defensively, reaching up to pet her own head. Every time she went to bed at night she still worried that somehow, when she awoke the next morning, the curls she detested so much would be back to torture her—like a monster in a fairy tale. "Why?" she asked suspiciously. "Don't you like it?"

"It's . . . fine," Nanna said cautiously, peering closer. "But, Casey, honey—do you think it's really *you*?"

"Who knows?" Casey sighed. "At least I don't have to spend two hours in the bathroom every morning trying to make myself presentable anymore."

"Thank God for *that*," Nanna said dryly, a twinkle enlivening her blue eyes. "Now, let's get back to the gossip!" She rubbed her papery hands together in undisguised anticipation.

"Well—you know that guy Drew who I've been hanging out with?" Casey said slowly, her hair momentarily forgotten.

"Is *that* what you kids call it these days?" Nanna snorted, sticking the spoon into the ice cream and pulling out a huge chunk. "In my day it was called *dating*," she said, popping the ice cream into her mouth and closing her eyes as it melted. "Or keeping company."

Casey giggled, licking vanilla ice cream off her freckled hand. "No offense, Nanna, but your day was like a million years ago."

"Don't I know it, honey," Nanna said, sighing dramatically before passing the spoon to Casey. "So, did this young man do something stupid?"

"Not exactly." Casey plunged the spoon back into the ice cream, waiting for it to soften up a bit more. "It's complicated."

"I've got all night," Nanna said, prying off another chunk of ice cream and putting it in her mouth with a smack of her lips. "Since Arthur canceled our date, I'm a free agent." Arthur was a retired Navy captain that Nanna had been seeing for about a month—almost as long as she'd been with Drew.

Casey pulled her bare knees up to her chest, resting her feet on the seat of the wooden chair, wrapping her arms around her knees. "Well, Drew has this ex-girlfriend, Madison."

"You mean Madison Macallister?" Nanna inquired, swallowing hard. "The same Madison Macallister who lives directly above us in the penthouse?"

"The *very* same," Casey said dryly, exhaling loudly. "And I think he still likes her. I was over at his place today helping him with this film he's making about rich kids on the Upper East Side, and he couldn't seem to keep his eyes off her—even when I left the room and didn't come back."

"It sounds to me like this Drew character might just be the kind of boy who can't keep what he really wants straight," Nanna said, poking a large-knuckled finger into Casey's knee intermittently for emphasis.

"I guess not," Casey said, wrapping her hand around her Nanna's. Her grandmother's hands were something that she had always loved. Holding them made her feel like a child again, sitting on Nanna's lap and playing with the larger veins that stood up in relief under her weathered skin. Grabbing a hold of her Nanna's hands now made her feel so much better—better than the cherry and vanilla ice-cream madness she had been shoving down her throat. "I think he thinks he wants me, but at the same time, he thinks he's supposed to want Madison. Or at least that's what everyone *else* thinks," Casey continued, her brain so overworked by all the thinking about Drew thinking about thinking that she felt it would surely explode.

"Well, I'll tell you what *I* think," Nanna said, squeezing Casey's hand with a strong, reassuring grip that belied the age and wear of her joints. "I think that this boy needs to be taught a lesson; needs to be shown a bit of humility. He needs to know that you know that he's not the *only* rich, young, smart, attractive and eligible young man on the Upper East Side."

"And how would I go about doing that? Based on what I know of the Meadowlark student body and the price of an iced soy milk latte at the coffee kiosk," Casey said throwing her arms into the air, the panic of her voice making her gestures seem just *that* much wilder, "I don't think there's *anyone* who's not *worth* dating around here, so to speak. Except for me, that is. So what am I supposed to do?"

Nanna laughed around the silver spoon that was carrying a decidedly ungrandmother-sized bite of ice cream into her small, rose-colored, grandmother-sized mouth. "Aren't you going to some fancy shindig next weekend?"

"I have no idea what a 'shindig' might be," Casey said with faux confusion. "I'm going to Sophie's sweet sixteen on Saturday—but that's a whole other problem. Did I tell you that it's going to be part of that show *My Spoiled Sweet Sixteen*?"

"My spoiled . . . *what*?" Nanna mumbled, her mouth full of ice cream.

"You are *such* an ice-cream hog," Casey said, prying the spoon from Nanna's hand.

Nanna patted her tiny, round stomach, grinning widely. "How *else* do you expect me to keep my girlish figure?"

Casey rolled her eyes, digging her spoon into the half-empty pint, holding the rapidly melting ice cream poised before her open mouth. "So, *My Spoiled Sweet Sixteen* is this reality show on the Pulse Network where a TV crew follows around a bunch of ridiculously overprivileged socialites as they plan their sweet sixteen parties."

"It sounds, quite possibly, like the worst show on television," Nanna said, placing the cover on the ice cream firmly. "That's about enough of you!" she admonished the half-empty carton with a wagging finger.

"It's pretty close," Casey said grabbing onto the container in mock horror and holding it to her chest protectively. "It makes me feel all dirty inside whenever I watch it. But more important, I was still eating that!"

"Not anymore," Nanna said briskly, standing up and

snatching the ice cream from Casey's grip, and placing it back in the freezer. As the freezer door closed, releasing a cloud of smoke into the air, Nanna turned around to face Casey, her hands on her hips.

"So this party will be on television? Well, that doesn't seem so bad to me." Nanna said thoughtfully, leaning over the gray-speckled kitchen counter and resting her bony elbows on the granite surface. "And I *still* think you should give this Drew fellow a taste of his own medicine—dance with someone else, walk around and flirt a little!" Nanna stood up, throwing her arms in the air exasperatedly. "That's what you're *supposed* to be doing at your age!"

"Then why are *you* still doing it at *your* age?" Casey asked innocently, raising her eyebrows.

"You're only as old as you feel," Nanna snapped, waving her hand dismissively before standing up straight, both hands massaging the small of her back beneath her white cashmere sweater.

"Then I must be a hundred and fifty," Casey said despondently, one finger tracing the gouges and knots in the wooden surface of the kitchen table. Ugh—she hated it when she sat around moping and feeling sorry for herself, but sometimes it just felt like no matter what she did, that the Madisons of the world would always win. Girls like Madison would always end up in the spotlight—with the Caseys of the world forever delegated to the background. She knew, even now, that at Sophie's party she'd most likely end up a nameless party guest, while Madison shone in the spotlight. Sometimes Casey felt like she'd never be that girl with the perfect boyfriend, the perfect life—it would always be Madison that everyone else wanted to be or be *with*. And that thought, when she allowed herself to think it, was depressing beyond belief.

"Oh, cheer up," Nanna said with a chuckle. "It could be worse—believe me. When Arthur came over last week he fell asleep on the couch in there like he was home in front of his own TV!" Nanna harrumphed, her hands back on her hips, indignant at the thought of her retired Navy captain boyfriend's obvious narcolepsy—or senility. *And at their age, let's face it, what's the difference?* Casey thought with a smile.

"What did you *expect* him to do—throw you to the living room floor and make passionate love to you or something?" Casey shuddered at the thought—good thing she usually made it a habit to go out when Arthur came over . . .

"Don't be silly." Nanna snorted. "I have no time for any funny business—we were *supposed* to be playing backgammon!" She walked out of the room, shaking her head from side to side and muttering under her breath. "Give him a taste of his own medicine, honey," Nanna yelled out before settling into the living room and picking up her knitting. From what Casey could tell from the amorphous red fuzzy ball, Nanna was either knitting a scarf, or some sort of weird, complicated doily. For her sake, she hoped it was the latter . . . the last thing she really needed at this point was to show up at Meadowlark all decked out in one of Nanna's "creations."

Casey got up with a sigh. If her life was one of the eighties movies she loved so much, Sophie's party really would be the time to make Drew jealous—except she wasn't sure you could actually make someone jealous who didn't even notice when you left the room . . . If her life were a movie, then Drew would've followed her out of his room yesterday, caught up with her in the hall before she even made it to the front door, and told her that Mad meant nothing to him. Then he would've tilted her head back with one hand, and pressed his soft lips to hers while his Ecuadorean maid looked on with tears in her eyes, a pot holder clutched in her hands. Fade out . . .

Casey walked down the hallway to her bedroom and pushed the door shut to drown out the sounds of Alex Trebek's annoying voice that told her that Nanna had begun her nightly ritual of watching *Jeopardy!* in the living room—at what some with normal hearing might consider a deafening volume. She pulled her cell phone from her pocket, checking for missed calls, her heart sinking in her chest as she glanced at the blank screen. *Ring damnit*, she pleaded silently with the inanimate piece of machinery. It was so ironic—cell phones were supposed to make it easier for people to communicate with one another and, right now at least, she felt more estranged from Drew than ever.

Casey sat down on her bed, flipping open her MacBook and checking her e-mail. Predictably, her inbox was empty. She reached for her violin, propped up against the side of the bed, and picked up her bow with the other had, closing her eyes and drawing the bow across the strings in a sweet, slightly mournful melody that made her heart ache with unexpressed sadness. The first notes of Mendelssohn's Violin Concerto had barely rang out in the room when Casey lifted the bow from the strings, and placed the instrument carefully back down onto the floor. Sometimes playing made her feel better—she could forget everything wrong in her life and escape into the music like a dream she never wanted to wake up from—but today it just wasn't working.

Instead, she pulled her MacBook into her lap and opened iTunes, which was set on random, and immediately skipped to a song by Paramore—whiny, angsty, ihatemyboyfriend music— sadly, the perfect soundtrack to this scene in the movie of her life. And that was definitely the problem with Drew. As awesome as he was most of the time, he clearly didn't understand nor recognize his responsibilities as the romantic lead in *her* movie. She played her part in his, and it was time for him to step up and do the same, but that didn't seem likely to happen anytime soon. So maybe Nanna, for once, was right—maybe the only way to make him realize they were starring in their own personal teen romance was to cast someone else in the lead.

needles
and
pins

"It's showtime, folks," Sophie whispered into the mirror, turning around to study her made-to-order Yves Saint Laurent ivory silk pantsuit, the hem of her pants studded with silver pins. There was nothing more seventies than the pantsuit, and during the lost decade of sex, drugs, and disco, YSL had practically redefined the concept of menswear on women, creating long, lean, and impossibly fitted silk suits for women. The impeccable tailoring meant your legs looked longer than usual, your stomach flatter, your shoulders ramrod straight. Basically, these suits made normal women look as glamorous and thin as fashion models. And with her custom ivory fedora cocked to the side, Sophie knew that this outfit was going to do more than rock her grand entrance at Marquee on Saturday night—as soon as her calfskin Balenciaga stiletto boots touched the red carpet, she knew she was going to be legendary.

The dressing room at Yves Saint Laurent was bigger than most New Yorkers' bedrooms, with pale gray carpeting and soft lighting that gave everyone's complexion a rosy glow in the full-length mirrors that covered the walls like sleek sheets of ice. But that glow had been replaced by the shriek of halogen lights, and the usual serene calm of the store was now a mess of noise and bustle as the Pulse crew plugged long ropes of extension cords into walls. Assistants carrying black cables roped around their arms walked briskly around the perimeter of the shop as the producer, a plump, fortyish redhead named Melanie, spoke incessantly into her cell phone with a voice that had all the subtlety of nails ripping down a blackboard. Sophie had been around the craziness of filming a reality TV show for about a week now—long enough to realize that anyone who chose to produce a show like this for a living was probably bordering on clinically insane. She wondered how her biological mother was able to stay grounded. Living with a camera stuck in your face, documenting your every move each time you left the house would probably drive you to craziness—or rehab—if it dragged on any longer than a few weeks.

Sophie turned around, inspecting the back of the suit in the mirror as the videographer, a cute, bearded guy named Mitch, mouthed "sorry" as he moved in for a closeup of her face. Sophie smiled for the camera, placing one hand on her waist and cocking a hip as she danced in front of the mirror. It was weird how totally comfortable she'd been in front of the camera ever since this whole sweet sixteen thing had begun. At first, she'd almost kind of been dreading it—the video crew, the relentless cameras following her around The Bram, to Randi's office, to her wardrobe fittings. She'd thought the minute the camera turned on that she'd freeze up, go blank. But the strange thing was that as soon as the lens pointed in her direction, she all but forgot it was even there at all. Maybe it was in her blood—after all, her mother was one of the most famous movie stars in the entire world . . .

"Sophie, can we have you try on the dress?" Melanie barked, looking harassed by the wireless headset clipped to one ear half-hidden by a tangle of red curls. For Sophie's grand entrance, she was planning to wear a vintage Halston gown in metallic gold that fell to her ankles and plunged down almost to the crack of her ass in the back, leaving a mile of skin exposed. It expressed Sophie's personal style perfectly: It was demure from the front, and very, very naughty in back.

"Actually, Melanie, I'd rather not," Sophie said, turning around to face her. "I want to keep it a surprise until the party."

Melanie shot her an annoyed look, badly camouflaged by a tight smile. "Fine. Whatever." Melanie turned toward the crew, motioning with one hand. "Let's move into the other room then, guys. Sophie, are you ready to show your friends *this* outfit?"

"No problem," Sophie said sweetly, turning and giving her suit one last once-over before walking out into the spacious glass- and light-filled showroom, placing the hat atop her head. Sophie never saw any reason to be rude about things—you caught more flies with honey than vinegar. And she had found over the years that the calmer she stayed in the midst of a stressful situation, the more unreasonable everyone else ended up looking. Madison, Phoebe, and Casey lounged on a long, buttery soft gray suede sofa, half-read issues of *In Style* and *Vogue* discarded and tossed onto the polished hardwood floor at their feet.

"So, guys," Sophie said as she made her grand entrance, her Balenciaga boots clicking authoritatively. "What do you think?" Madison, Phoebe, and Casey looked over at the same time, Phoebe jumping to her feet in excitement, her ballet flats sliding soundlessly across the floor.

"You look amazing!" Phoebe exclaimed, rushing over and grabbing Sophie's hand, her eyes sweeping her outfit appreciatively. "That suit is the bomb!"

"It's the hotness," Casey agreed, walking over and squeezing Sophie's arm through the satiny silk jacket. Who was this freckly person resembling Casey McCloy? Casey never said things like "the hotness." *It's about time*, Sophie thought, walking over to Mad, who was still lounging on the couch, her booted feet tucked beneath her. *Now if we could just do something about her clothes, we'd be in business . . .*

"What do you think, Mad?" Sophie asked proudly, doing a pirouette, her hands on her hips.

"It's so hot it's practically nuclear," Mad said, her green eyes glittering. "I feel like such a backseat buyer right now." Mad smiled her slow, catlike smile, grinning into the camera and then dropping her eyes bashfully to the floor. A backseat buyer was someone who got totally jazzed over someone else's purchases. *If Madison's a backseat buyer*, Sophie thought suspiciously, *then Casey's the Queen of England* . . .

Sophie threw Madison a smile, but inside, she was more than just a little confused. What the hell was wrong with Mad lately? *It's like Invasion of the Socialite Snatchers around here*, Sophie thought, walking over to a full-length mirror. A manipulative, scheming Madison, she could take. A sniping, bitchy Madison—that was just a typical day. But a nice, supportive Madison was just too much for Sophie to bear. And ever since she'd become the next big thing, Madison had been acting almost disgustingly, cloyingly sweet—not to mention humble. And in Sophie's opinion, Madison Macallister and humble went together about as well as milk and orange juice . . .

Maybe stardom's changed her for the better, Sophie thought as she adjusted the fedora so it dipped more deeply over her left eye. Sophie supposed that theoretically Madison's attitude adjustment was definitely preferable to the barbs and insults Mad usually sprinkled through their conversations. But, the longer the niceness went on, the more she found herself kind of missing the way Mad used to be. Watching Madison act so nice to everyone made Sophie feel a little queasy—like she'd been transported to another planet where everyone held hands and sang Kum By Yah while drinking soy milk. *Or maybe it's just for the cameras*, Sophie thought, her lips curving into a smirk. Knowing Madison, that explanation would be a lot more likely . . .

Sophie walked back over to the couch and sat down next to Mad, smoothing the silky material of the trousers, the cameraman moving closer to get the both of them in a two-shot. As perfect as she knew everything would be on Saturday, Sophie was starting to get more and more nervous about the prospect of meeting her mother—and there was no way she could keep it to herself any longer. Since Mad was being so nice lately, Sophie figured that now was as good a time as any to let her in on the big news.

"Are you excited?" Mad asked, squeezing Sophie's hand supportively.

"Beyond." Sophie giggled, tucking her hair behind her ears. "And for more than one reason."

"What do you mean?" Mad asked, dropping her voice and leaning slightly closer.

Sophie felt the words she had been dying to speak catch in her throat—a secret for too long, they were hard-pressed to come out. Breathing in deeply, she looked away from Madison and from the camera just in time to catch Casey and Phoebe, as they held up copies of fashion magazines to their faces like masks, and proceeded to walk around the clothes racks like zombies. The sight of her two friends acting like such complete crazies in one of the chicest stores in Manhattan made a torrent of giggles rise up from the pit of Sophie's stomach, and in trying to keep them down, those other, secret words spilled out.

"A few weeks ago my parents told me . . . that I'm adopted."

Madison's face froze into a perfect, beautiful mask, her features as white and smooth as a vat of vanilla ice cream. "No shit," she whispered, squeezing Sophie's arm more tightly. "Are you okay about it?"

Madison asking if she was okay was about as weird as Yves Saint Laurent coming back from the dead to pin her pantsuit himself. Sophie tried to ignore the fact that her best friend had clearly become a pod person, and took a deep breath before continuing. Why was this still so uncomfortable to talk about? She'd told the Pulse bigwigs and Casey so far—shouldn't saying "I'm adopted" out loud be getting easier at this point?

"I guess," Sophie shrugged, avoiding Madison's gaze, "but that's not the weirdest part. My bio mom . . . is Melissa Von Norton."

Madison's green eyes widened. "Are you *kidding* me?" she said breathily. "She's like my favorite actress in the whole *world!*"

"You and everyone else," Sophie said, surprising even herself with how totally jaded she already sounded. *Have I become just another Hollywood brat already?* she wondered, crossing one leg over the other.

"Have you talked to her?" Mad asked, uncurling her feet from underneath her and crossing her legs, leaning in toward Sophie, the camera momentarily forgotten.

"Yeah, that's the thing . . ." Sophie said weakly, realizing all at once that she was in over her head. Up until this moment she hadn't let herself see how much she had riding on this one night—a night that had to end perfectly for so many reasons she'd recently lost count. As she looked into Mad's expectant face—and at the camera lens placed inches from her own—the emotional dam she'd built so carefully since she found out that she wasn't technically Sophie St. John broke open, her thoughts flooding with all the doubt she'd been pushing to the back of her mind. Would Melissa even recognize her? And even if, by some miracle, they did happen to get along, Sophie couldn't help but be worried that her mother might not stick around to get to know her at all. Even if they wound up bonding over a few cosmopolitans, Sophie knew that it didn't necessarily mean that her mother would want to have an actual *relationship* with her or anything. And in her darkest moments, Sophie couldn't stop herself from wondering if the party was going to be just a one-shot deal . . .

"*What?*" Madison snapped, rolling her eyes, and the reassuringly sharp tone of her voice silenced the thoughts crowding Sophie's brain, and brought her back to reality.

"She's coming to the party," Sophie said. "I'm meeting her for the first time on Saturday night."

"Holy expectations, Batman," Mad breathed. "Way to pile on the pressure."

"*Exactly,*" Casey chimed in, a long white silk scarf draped artlessly around her neck, her face hidden by a pair of black shades that were so huge, it made her head look like a peanut.

"You are a walking fashion violation," Madison snapped, then helplessly burst into laughter at the sight of her.

"Tell me something I *don't* know," Casey said, laughing as she pushed the sunglasses on top of her head and pulled on a pair of black leather elbow-length gloves. "Do you think these are too much?"

"On you?" Sophie giggled as Casey held her arms out in front of her. "Definitely."

Phoebe walked over, holding a pair of beige, calfskin ankle boots, the supple leather gleaming in the light. "These *better* come in my size," she muttered, doubling over with laughter as she caught sight of Casey's outfit. "I can't leave you alone for five seconds," she exclaimed, snatching the sunglasses from Casey's head and trying them on herself, blowing air kisses into the mirror like a French film star—which, of course, was basically what Phoebe thought she was anyway.

"Oh my God," Madison deadpanned. "Those work on *no one*. They're like a black hole of good taste."

"I kind of like them," Sophie said meekly, glad that attention had been diverted away from the party—and her mother.

As if on cue, Mad turned to Phoebe, smiling brilliantly. "Sophie was just telling me that she's adopted." Madison turned back to Sophie, an innocent look plastered all over her face—a look Sophie had seen a million times before—and one that she could see right through. *Guess the honeymoon's over*, Sophie thought, watching as Madison went in for the kill. "It's not a secret anymore, is it?" Mad gestured at the camera, her emerald ring flashing in the light. "I mean, it's going to be on TV and everything anyway . . ."

Sophie shrugged, heat breaking over her skin like a creeping forest fire as Phoebe stared at her uncomprehendingly.

"And the best part is," Mad continued, her voice picking up speed as she raced to get to the good part of the story. "Her biological mother is *Melissa Von Norton!*"

"And she's coming to the party on Saturday!" Casey said excitedly, grabbing onto Phoebe's arm.

"Wow," Phoebe said slowly, taking in the news slowly, the way she processed everything. "That's totally *Outer Limits*." Phoebe looked as bemused as if someone had suddenly smacked her in the face with a banana cream pie. Sophie watched as the boots Phoebe'd been lusting after so hard only moments before slipped to the floor with a clatter.

"How did *you* know that?" Madison asked, turning her attention to Casey, her voice the very definition of a cold front.

"Uh, I kind of told her already," Sophie said apologetically, trying to brush it off like it was no big deal, and watching as Madison's expression froze like water on an icy cold windowpane.

"You told her before *me*? Or even *Phoebe*?" Madison asked in disbelief, looking away from the camera, shaking her hair out of her eyes with a toss of her head. As Sophie scrambled for an answer, she gradually became aware that the Pulse crew was motionless, hanging on their every word.

"Umm . . . well . . ." Sophie stuttered, staring at the floor, the ceiling—anything to avoid having to look into her best friend's eyes. "*Kind* of."

"Oh my God, this means you'll totally get to go to Hollywood on breaks—maybe even on location with her!" Phoebe chimed in, breaking the tension in the air. "You're going to have so much fun!"

Sophie smiled, trying to look excited, but any joy she felt about finally being able to tell her friends about her mom was spoiled by the fact that Madison was undoubtedly pissed off at her.

"Well, I should go," Madison said brusquely, sliding her shades over her eyes and standing up. "I have to meet Antonio at The London—he's bringing my test shots."

Phoebe raised her eyebrows, clearly impressed.

"Wow," she said, "he's taking you to Gordon Ramsey's

restaurant just to go over test shots? Oh my God, he's totally in love with you!" Phoebe let out a squeal that sounded more like rubber tires on asphalt to Sophie than an expression of joy.

Madison—in her typical bitchy fashion—ignored Phoebe's outburst, throwing her black quilted Chanel tote over her shoulder with a flip of the wrist that let Sophie know she was definitely pissed off, a secret smile playing at the corners of her reglossed lips. "We're meeting in the bar, for your information," she snapped. "Models don't eat anyway."

"True dat." Sophie sighed, looking down at her flat stomach lying beneath her silk trousers. "I want to lose two more pounds by Saturday."

"Why?" Phoebe laughed. "So you can blow away in a sudden wind?"

"No . . ." Sophie drawled, "so that I look the total package when I meet my new mom."

"Oh my God." Madison groaned, rolling her eyes toward the discreet gray spotlights adorning the ceiling. "I'm out of here."

Sophie watched as Mad walked out the front door of YSL without looking back, throwing a jaunty wave over one shoulder, her black cashmere wrap fluttering in the breeze. Mad would get over it—she always did. And besides, Sophie didn't have time to worry about whether or not Mad would forgive her—she had more important things to obsess about right now—like whether or not her mother would show up on Saturday night at all. And even if she did, what on *earth* would she actually say to her? "Hi, Mom. Nice to meet you. I loved that scene you did with Brad Pitt in that film?" It wasn't as if finding out you've been adopted and meeting your biological mother was exactly easy in the first place, but when she was so damn famous that she was in every movie, on the cover of every magazine—not to mention the fact that everyone on the planet was strangely, distantly familiar with her life—how was a girl supposed to deal with that? A pantsuit was a start, to be sure. It would, she hoped, be the best costume for the day. But the hand-stitched silk was unfortunately mute and devoid of advice.

The cameras and lights were circling in around her after capturing Madison's departure—the producers were beyond delighted that one of her best friends had a burgeoning modeling career. She highly doubted that they would've followed Casey or Phoebe down the street. Behind the lights, she could see Melanie holding up a dry-erase board with the words STOP LOOKING SO SAD scrawled across the surface in black, frenetic strokes. It felt so strange having the Pulse cameras, the lights, Melanie's signs, all there to witness these days leading up to the party. She imagined it would almost be easier not being herself in front of the camera—acting, playing a part, like her mother, with all the words written out for you ahead of time by people who knew all the right things to say at all the right times. She'd only have to memorize her lines.

my london, london bridge wanna go down . . .

Madison stepped into the bar at The London, her kitten-heeled, green suede pumps clicking musically across the hardwood floor. Madison walked briskly, still smarting from Sophie's obvious friendship faux pas. She was going to have to do *something* about Casey—that had become totally clear. In the course of less than two months, this clueless loser had not only stolen her boyfriend, but now had basically hijacked her witless, unsuspecting friends too. Was their no end to the humiliation she had to suffer at the hands of this terminally unfashionable Midwestern parasite?

Apparently not.

But as mad as she was at Sophie at the moment, Madison knew that Sophs was just too nice and too dumb to be able to see through Casey's goody-goody act the way she could. Madison stopped in front of a large, oval silver mirror, checking her lip gloss, and pulling her tube of Mac's Oh Baby Lipglass from her chocolate brown Gucci Hobo, swiping the wand across her already sticky lips to calm her nerves. The thought of having to look at the photographic train wreck that would surely be her test shots didn't exactly make her want to start jumping up and down or anything—and the knowledge that she would soon be looking at herself in those photographs, so stiff and nervous, made her shiver as she stopped at the entrance to the heavily air-conditioned bar and looked around.

As much as she hated the idea, she was going to have to tell Antonio that, even though she appreciated his offer, she just didn't think she wanted to be a model after all. The thought of using her body to sell things, whether it was a tube of toothpaste or a Bulgari necklace, made her feel like she was nothing more than a pretty exterior—expensive, but definitely disposable. If there was one thing Madison Macallister knew better than anyone else, it was that if you weren't the one in control, you were probably the one being manipulated. And Madison made it her personal mission to never, ever be the one who was being played—for any reason. Besides, she just didn't like feeling out of control—it made her feel all oogey and sweaty . . .

The London was full of leggy, glamorous Upper East Siders lounging on high-backed bar stools in fashionable frocks, their legs dropping coolly to the floor like long-stemmed white lilies, cocktail glasses full of clear liquid held between their manicured fingers. Gordon Ramsey's newest venture had practically redefined the concept of Upper East Side luxury, with its mirror-paneled dining room, and five-hundred-and-fifty-dollar sidecar—a cocktail so totally elite that it wasn't even written on the menu—and featured Hennessy Ellipse super premium cognac and Grand Marnier 150 poured from a decanter specially designed by Thomas Bastide of Baccarat.

Waiters clad head-to-toe in black walked languorously though the expansive space, silver trays balanced in their hands. The room was patterned in subdued shades of cream and black, and Madison's green eyes scanned the dimly lit bar area for Antonio, who was seated at the bar wearing a sleek, charcoal gray suit with a cobalt blue silk tie, speaking rapidly on his cell phone. A cut-crystal tumbler of amber liquid sat in front of him on the bar, the deep cherry wood polished to a rich, satiny brilliance. His lips curved into a smile as his dark eyes fixed on hers, raising one hand in greeting as he snapped his cell phone shut.

"*Cara,* how are you?" he asked, his voice a low, seductive purr as he leaned in to kiss her warmly on both cheeks, the lemony scent of his cologne sticking to her hair, her skin. "I was beginning to worry," he said, pushing up one dark sleeve so that a D&G watch with an alligator band shone in the soft light drifting overhead.

Madison sat down on a bar stool, crossing her legs beneath the forest green and caramel patterned wrap dress she wore. "Sorry I'm late—I had to stop home and change."

Antonio raised one hand, signaling at the bartender. "The lady will have . . ." He turned to face her, his teeth glowing in his tanned face as he smiled. "What will you have?"

"A Negroni," Mad said casually, as if she ordered them all the time. She'd heard some actress order one in an old movie from the sixties she saw on TV one night last spring when she couldn't sleep. It always sounded good, but she had no fucking idea what, exactly, was in one—for all she knew it could be some revolting mix of peach schnapps and battery acid. Whatever—she'd deal. As long as she looked good while holding it, she could choke down anything—even if it ended up tasting like ass.

"You look gorgeous, *cara*, just perfect," Antonio purred as he sipped his cocktail, his dark eyes traveling over the length of her body.

"Antonio, you say that every time I *see* you," Madison said flirtatiously as the bartender set a brilliant red drink before her, ice cubes clinking against the tall glass.

"That is because it is true," Antonio answered back, holding his drink up to hers. "A toast," he said, staring into her eyes, "to the most beautiful girl on the Upper East Side—and soon," he added, "the whole world."

Madison's stomach dropped as their glasses clinked, as much from the intensity of Antonio's stare as the feeling that being a model wasn't what she wanted after all. When she'd left Sam's studio last week, all she'd wanted to do was hide under a rock until the next millennium. The whole experience had left such a bad taste in her mouth that she wasn't sure she wanted to step in front of the camera ever again—much less become the modeling world's next big thing. Forget the whole control thing—there was something distinctly cheap about the whole experience of being a model, and if Madison Macallister was anything at all, it *certainly* wasn't cheap . . .

Antonio picked up a large white envelope from the bar in

front of him, pulling out sheets of glossy, photographic paper. "I want to show you something," he said gravely, tapping the sheets of paper against the bar for emphasis.

"Antonio, look," Madison said, sweat beginning to break out under her arms, "Sam and I didn't really—"

"Shhh . . ." Antonio said softly, pressing a finger to her lips. At the soft touch of his hand, Madison went as limp as a kitten. "It is not important," he finished as she fell silent, leaning in to stroke her cheek with his fingers. *Goddamnit*, Madison thought with no small measure of annoyance, *what is going on? Will this guy kiss me already!* She leaned in slightly, parting her lips, waiting for the touch of his lips on hers. She was so close to his golden skin . . .

But just as she closed her eyes completely, she felt a rush of wind as Antonio slapped the contact sheets down on the bar in front of her with a harsh, thwacking sound. "Take a look at these, *cara*. They are magnificent, no?"

Madison warily opened her eyes, her annoyance fading completely as she stared down at the contact sheets. Each small frame of film held a miniature Madison in its center, her white-blond hair shining in the light. Her body looked long and lean, her limbs as sculpted as if she spent every day at the gym, subsisting on nothing but energy bars and air—which she definitely did *not*. Her eyes looked knowingly into the camera, and even in the shots where she was obviously uncomfortable there was something compelling about her stance, the determination in her green eyes slicing through the lens.

"I can't believe that's really *me*," Madison murmured in disbelief, reaching out and tracing her own image with the tip of one finger, pulling the contact sheets closer to take a better look. "I thought it was a total disaster. I mean, Sam and I didn't exactly become best friends or anything and—"

"What he thinks does not matter," Antonio said, waving a hand dismissively. "What matters is what the *camera* thinks—and it is clearly in love with you."

"I guess," Madison stammered, "but I don't really know *how* to model, and I'm just not really sure I want to do this after all." Madison pushed the contact sheets away and took a deep breath, tapping her heel against the bar stool nervously. Before she walked into the restaurant, she'd all but convinced herself that she was going to turn Antonio down—the shoot was such a disaster and she didn't relish the prospect of doing another one any time soon. So she'd managed to kick Sam where it hurt—so what? At the end of the day, there would always be some other photographer trying to get into her pants, some other random guy who thought that just because she was a model she was dumb and easy. Dumb—maybe sometimes. But easy? Never. *After all*, Madison thought, picking up her Negroni and making a face when the bitter liquor hit her tongue, *a girl's got to draw the line somewhere . . .*

"Listen to me, *cara*." Antonio said, taking her hand in his own. When his hand touched hers, Madison felt herself go all limp—just like the alligator she saw on Animal Planet last week who rolled over, completely vegged-out and hypnotized because some animal expert rubbed its scaly belly in the right spot. If this is what it felt like when Antonio so much as touched her hand, she was definitely in real trouble if he ever so much as grazed her belly with *one* of his fingers. She'd probably fall into some kind of a lust-induced coma, only to wake in twenty years, first asking for Antonio—and then a Diet Coke . . .

"Madison, *cara*, you were *born* for this." Antonio caressed her palm, shivers radiating from her hand all the way down to her spine—she felt like her vertebrae were melting right into her chair. "You must reconsider. What can I do to convince you?" he asked, his dark eyes sparkling.

"Well, I don't know . . ." Madison demurred, sensing an opportunity to make Antonio an offer he couldn't refuse—and why would he want to anyway? If she really was as gorgeous as everyone was telling her, he should be fairly panting to take things to the next level. But since the whole fiasco with Drew, Mad knew that her confidence just wasn't what it had once been. Drew's rejection hurt more than she would ever let on to anyone else—even admitting it to herself stung like a shaving nick, one that wouldn't stop bleeding all over the place. . . . "My friend's having a party at Marquee this Saturday night. Be my date and I'll *think* about it."

Antonio smiled, lifting her hand to his lips and kissing it softly before releasing her. "It would be my pleasure to accompany you," he said, his eyes never leaving her face.

"I'm not promising anything, Antonio," she warned, her face serious. "I *still* haven't talked to my mother about all this," she added, taking another tiny sip of the noxious Negroni and pushing it away, scowling like a pouty baby. It really wouldn't hurt to string Antonio along a little longer, Mad told herself. And showing up at Sophie's party with Antonio at her side would definitely rocket her reputation into the stratosphere—not that her reputation really needed any help in the first place . . .

"Perhaps she will be there Saturday night?" Antonio asked, downing the rest of his drink, which, for his sake, she hoped tasted a hell of a lot better than her own—and signaled the bartender for the check.

"Unfortunately," Madison said, "but I can't promise she'll be, umm, particularly *coherent* or anything."

"I look forward to meeting her," Antonio said with a chuckle, placing a platinum Amex on top of the check and handing it to the bartender. "If she is anywhere as beautiful as you, I'm sure I will recognize her immediately."

Madison snorted, rolling her eyes. "Yeah, she's all right— except she's about a million years old!" Madison stood up, smoothing down her dress.

"I will pick you up in my car, yes?" Antonio asked, sliding his Burberry trench coat from the back of the chair and slinging it over one arm.

Yes, yes, yes, Madison thought while nodding happily, unable to keep her eyes from noticing his perfectly square jaw, or the fact that his dark eyelashes were about a foot long. *Why do guys always have the longest lashes?* Madison pondered, trying to distract herself from thinking the usual lust-filled daydreaming that occupied her brain when she was around Antonio, pushing rational thoughts to a tiny, dust-filled corner in the back of her skull.

"Eight o'clock?" she asked as her cell phone began to buzz noisily. Madison reached into the pocket of her shearling coat and pulled out her cell, the word EDIE flashing across the tiny screen. Looking at her phone in undisguised annoyance, Madison switched off the ringer, throwing it back into her pocket.

She'd wait until she was safely outside before calling her back—there was nothing worse than looking like an infant whose mother still kept tabs on her in front of a guy she was trying to impress. And, more than anything, Madison wanted Antonio to be impressed. Not only was he unbelievably gorgeous, but she knew that bringing him to Sophie's party as her date would drive Drew completely over the edge. And then she'd have him right where she wanted him . . . completely tortured—a jealous, hormonally ridden, angsty nightmare of seething regret—which could only be seen as totally unattractive to a certain newly straightened Midwest moron . . .

"Until then," Antonio said, leaning in and kissing her on both cheeks, his lips lingering just a touch too long on either side of her face, applying pressure that was both gentle and firm. Madison closed her eyes at his touch, already planning the drop-dead gorgeous outfit she'd surely find to wear on Saturday night . . .

that's entertainment

Phoebe stepped into The Bramford's first-floor entertainment lounge, swinging the heavy oak door shut behind her and switching on the lights. The lounge had once been one of The Bram's most popular amenities, featuring a giant movie screen, state-of-the-art popcorn machine, and an enormous, adjacent, sculptured outdoor garden that nannies mostly used for picnics in the summer months. But since most of the current tenants had apartments equipped with their *own* private screening rooms, and, being October, it was way too chilly for picnics anymore, the lounge was mostly deserted at this time of year—not to mention this late at night.

Phoebe flopped down on an enormous black leather couch. The fawn-colored Christian Louboutin knee-high boots she'd stolen from Madeline's closet earlier were tucked into a pair of faded jeans. The room was empty and quiet, and Phoebe shivered, crossing her denim-clad legs, and pulling her black cardigan tighter around her body, the edges of a robin's egg–blue camisole peeking out from the soft cashmere.

Phoebe looked around at the room, with its floor-to-ceiling windows covering one wall, and the plush red velvet curtains surrounding the movie screen. At least once a month, The Bram Clan had a slumber party—of sorts. They would drag a pile of *Sex and the City* and *Footballers' Wives* DVDs down to the lounge and spend an entire evening watching one episode after another while painting each other's nails—and gossiping furiously, of course. Phoebe sighed, her heart racing. She knew this was total madness—anyone could walk in at any time, even Sophie, although, as caught up as she was in planning her upcoming party, it was highly unlikely. *What am I doing here?* Phoebe moaned inwardly, closing her eyes and leaning her head back on the soft leather as the door opened with a creak.

Phoebe sat up, the blood thudding in her veins as Jared entered the room wearing a navy blue sweater that looked so soft she immediately wanted to bury her face in it, and a pair of baggy jeans he'd belted tightly so that the blue and green plaid of his boxers showed over the waistband. Jared grinned happily at the prospect of finding her already there, and walked across the room with long, loping strides before sitting down beside her, pushing his dark hair from his eyes, picking up her hand and enfolding it in his own.

"Wow," he said, smiling. "You beat me here. You must've really wanted to see me."

Phoebe rolled her eyes and dropped his hand. "You wish,"

she snorted, looking away before the smile that was slowly creeping across her face completely took over. "I was just bored, so I came down here early."

"Yeah, right," Jared said, reaching over as lazily and calculated as a cat to take her hand once again. "And I changed my shirt seven times before coming down here because I was just *indecisive.*"

Phoebe laughed, turning to face him. When his blue eyes met hers, she knew that looking him straight in the face was definitely a bad idea—not to mention the obvious fact that within five minutes of walking into the room, he was holding her hand like he owned it. Looking at Jared was like being sucked into a spinning, dizzy vortex. If she looked at him for long enough, there was no telling what might happen. Did she really want to find out?

"I can't stop thinking about you," Jared said quietly, reaching over and smoothing the dark hair from her face. "And I'm not sure I want to." His lips moved closer and closer to hers, until she felt the warmth of them on her own, her mouth opening as she responded to his touch. As they continued to kiss, Phoebe felt herself falling backward until she was lying horizontally on the leather couch with Jared above her. Somehow, the weight of his body on hers, as delicious as it was, made her feel like things were moving too fast, spiraling out of control. She put her hands on his chest and pushed hard, sitting up and running a hand through her tangled hair.

"We can't do this," she said, breathing heavily and all at once overcome with fear. "It's *wrong.* We're wrong for doing it."

"Does it *feel* wrong to you?" Jared asked, exhaling loudly

and sitting up, his blue eyes glittering with impatience. "Because it doesn't to me. When I'm with you I feel like I'm exactly where I'm supposed to be."

Phoebe sat motionless, Jared's words hanging in the air between them. It may have been the nicest thing anyone had ever said to her in her life—anyone with a penis, that is. But it didn't change the fact that they were sneaking around, that despite her best intentions, she'd become nothing more than a carbon copy of her own mother: lying, orchestrating clandestine meetings, hurting the very people she was supposed to love. It had to stop—now. And if Jared wasn't going to make it stop, then Phoebe knew it was all up to her.

"I can't see you anymore," Phoebe said woodenly, stumbling to her feet and trying to ignore the aching pain that threatened to rip her chest apart as she walked toward the door.

"C'mon, Phoebe!" Jared said, jumping to his feet and following her. "Don't do this!" She could feel the warmth of his body as he stood behind her, his breath on the back of her neck, but she didn't dare turn around. As she stood there, she prayed that he wouldn't try to touch her—she knew that if she felt the warm pressure of his hands on her flesh, she'd turn around to face him, open her arms, and give in. *You're your mother's daughter all right*, she thought, her body trembling so hard she felt as if she were about to crack in two. *Weak, weak, weak . . .*

When she finally spoke, the voice that came out of her throat was hoarse, shaky, and not at all her own. "I have to," Phoebe said, turning the knob with one hand and walking out the door before Jared could say another word.

shake
your
groove
thing

Casey followed Phoebe down the red carpet in front of Marquee, stopping short as Phoebe paused at the entrance—which was currently blocked by a buffed-out, bare-chested guy holding a clipboard. He was dressed in a pair of red satin shorts, red-and-white athletic socks, and not much else, his blond hair hanging over his eyes, his exposed bare skin tanned to a buttery shade of caramel. Casey tried to smile as flashbulbs exploded in her face, the bright flashes of light causing red and green spots to appear in her line of vision.

Phoebe turned back to Casey, a wicked gleam in her eye. *Yummy*, she mouthed, rolling her eyes in the doorman's direction for further emphasis. Casey could barely hear herself think, what with all the noise from the screaming crowd of hangers-on and wanna-bes clamoring for entrance beyond the red velvet ropes, not to mention the insistent, pounding disco that was blasting from the club at such a pitch, they'd heard it from at least fifty feet away. The bass buzzed through the vintage Jordache jeans she'd found while rummaging through the bargain bin of a thrift store downtown called Cheap Jack's—and they were so unbelievably tight that they looked as if they were painted on. Earlier that evening, she'd been forced to get Nanna to wrestle the zipper into place with a pair of pliers as Casey lay faceup on the bed, gasping for air. *No wonder everyone smoked so much pot in the sixties and seventies,* Casey thought, as Nanna helped her up. You'd have to be very stoned indeed to forget the fact that the skintight denim was most certainly cutting off the blood flow to your brain . . .

The black tube top shot through with metallic gold thread that she wore and the pair of gold Jimmy Choo platform sandals on her feet were borrowed from Sophie's overstuffed closet. Casey tapped one of the shoes against the soft red carpet, trying to smile gracefully into the cameras, waiting for her head to explode from the relentless disco beat, the insistent shriek of whistles being blown from inside Marquee's dim interior. "Just keep them," Sophie had said offhandedly last night from the depth of her cavernous, grape-colored closet. As Casey had looked around at the shelves stuffed with designer purses—some with the tags still hanging off—she wondered for the millionth time since moving to the Upper East Side what it would be like to give away a six-hundred-dollar pair of shoes, just because you felt like it.

For her own sixteenth birthday last June, her mother had taken Casey and her best friend, Marissa, to Chicago for the weekend. They'd stayed in a swanky boutique hotel just off

Michigan Avenue, where the management provided goldfish bowls in the room in case you felt lonely during your stay. During the nightly wine-tasting in the lobby, Casey and Marissa had giggled over tiny sips of wine, then flailed around their room before dinner, pretending they were totally wasted. That whole weekend she'd felt so grown up, running around in the big city, the very picture of glamorous sophistication. But now, for the first time, she was painfully aware that next to Sophie's party, her birthday weekend might as well have taken place at Chuck E. Cheese.

And the situation with Drew was definitely not helping the matter any. They'd suddenly gone from hanging out every day to waving tentatively as they passed each other in the hallway. As excited as she'd been all week about Sophie's party, Casey couldn't shake the feeling that something between her and Drew had gone somehow horribly wrong. Ever since that afternoon they'd interviewed Madison for the documentary, he'd all but ignored her. When she'd first been invited to Sophie's sweet sixteen, she'd giddily assumed that Drew would ask her to go with him—like a real boyfriend. She'd lain on her bed and fantasized about standing on the brightly lit dance floor, her arms entwined with Drew's as they did the Hustle, a gardenia tucked behind her newly straightened hair, her white silk Oscar de la Renta dress whipping around her body. But as the days inched closer and closer to Saturday, it became suddenly, scarily clear that she'd be most likely arriving with Phoebe. *Damn Madison Macallister*, Casey thought grumpily. She was always showing up at the worst possible moment and ruining absolutely everything—just because she could.

The doorman winked at Phoebe and waved them through. Casey followed Phoebe's short, sparkling silver Versace dress into the club. *Only Phoebe could get away with a dress like that—anyone else would just look like a walking disco ball,* Casey thought with a smile as she entered Marquee, her eyes adjusting to the dimness and swirl of colored lights that swept the bar and the dance floor. With Phoebe's dark hair pulled back in a twist, a glittering Swarovski hair ornament in the shape of a flower pinned artfully in the back, Phoebe looked like a star that had somehow fallen out of the sky and landed in the middle of Manhattan. Next to Phoebe, Casey felt like an extra from the set of *Charlie's Angels* in her skintight jeans and top. She'd tried to feather her newly straightened hair, but it had weird bends and dips in it from Nanna's million-year-old brush and hairdryer set that were clearly as much of a relic from the seventies as Casey's jeans . . .

Casey stumbled as she tried to keep up with Phoebe's long strides, her Choos catching on the red carpet that extended into the cavernous space of the club as she fell to her knees with a resounding thud. *So much for making a grand entrance,* Casey thought bitterly as Phoebe turned around, holding out a hand for her to grab.

"Oh my God." Phoebe moaned good-naturedly. "I *so* don't know you right now."

"That carpet is *not* platform-friendly," Casey answered, her face flushing with heat as she brushed off her jeans with both hands, praying that nobody had seen her less-than-graceful entrance—especially the Pulse cameras—which were undoubtedly everywhere . . .

Phoebe squealed, grabbing Casey's arm and squeezing tightly with excitement as they looked around the room. "Her parents must be feeling *seriously* guilty," Phoebe said with a giggle.

Casey could only nod dumbly in agreement as she took in the giant silver crescent moon hanging from the ceiling— complete with a silver-clad go-go dancer riding astride it as it swung from one end of the dance floor to the other, her blond hair flying, her silver hot pants and high boots gleaming in the light. The scene beneath this discofied version of the dish, the spoon, and the cow jumping over the moon was no less spectacular. The room was packed with people, many clad in whites, pastels, and grays, the fabrics all likely smelling strongly of mothballs from the thirty-plus years since they'd seen the light of day, or, uh, a disco ball. But the crush of bodies and polyester was out of the closet, so to speak, limbs and hips moving to the four-four thump of old records, the silky strings and tinny synthesizers escalating to a fever pitch.

"Hey," Phoebe said, her eyes having landed on a familiar-looking poof of white-blond hair, "there's Warhol over there . . . and Edie Sedgwick, too!" She pointed in the direction of the dance floor, but Casey saw nothing except the artfully muscled flank of a gigantic white horse—one of five trotting about the room—its mane doused in silver and gold glitter, a disco cowgirl riding sidesaddle on its sparkling back.

"Warhol, horses, shirtless boys—this party is beyond ridiculous. Imma get my mingle on!" Phoebe cried with joy, one hand grabbing tightly onto Casey's arm and dragging her off into the crowd toward a white spotlight near the bar. As Phoebe and Casey approached the bar, Melanie rushed up to them, grabbing Casey by the arm and sighing with pent-up exasperation.

"There you two are," she said triumphantly, her red curls springing wildly around her head, making Casey grateful once again that her hair was now silky straight. Casey raised one hand to her head reflexively, smoothing down her yellow hair that now fell almost to her shoulders.

"Will you *stop* petting yourself like you're a prize pony?" Phoebe laughed, slapping Casey's hand away from her head.

"Sorry to interrupt such an important conversation," Melanie said sarcastically, "but you girls have to come in the back so we can mike you for the show."

"We have to wear microphones?" Casey asked, yelling over the blaring music streaming from the speakers directly overhead.

"How *else* do you expect anyone to hear you?" Melanie said, clearly annoyed. "And where's your other friend—the model?"

"We haven't seen her yet," Phoebe shouted over the din. "But knowing Mad she'll probably get here just before midnight—she's always late," Phoebe explained as a pair of hands snaked over her eyes from behind, and the crisp, floral scent of Marc Jacobs Blush perfume wafted through the air. Even if Casey had been struck suddenly blind, she'd still have known Madison was in the immediate vicinity—and the scent of her perfume, so delicious and innocuous on every other occasion, was now rapidly making Casey feel unbelievably nauseated. *Or maybe you just don't like Madison Macallister very much*, her inner bitch said smugly, as Casey tried to smile.

"What's up?" Madison inquired, her green eyes outlined in electric blue liquid liner, the top lids sparkling with Urban Decay eyeshadow in Chopper, the copper flecks embedded in the shiny powder catching the light. "Is this intense or what?" Madison, of course, looked stunning as usual in a cream, vintage Halston gown that featured a plunging V of a neckline that exposed about a mile of tanned bare skin. *How is she even keeping her, umm, goodies inside that thing?* Casey wondered, trying to surreptitiously take a better look. Did she use double-stick tape? Staples? Krazy Glue? Or maybe the gown just stayed up from the sheer gravity of Madison's presence, the supernatural force that was Madison Macallister . . .

Before Casey or Phoebe could even begin to shout over the music, Madison turned to a tall, dark-haired man standing behind her and grabbed him by the hand, pulling him into the center of the group. "Phoebe, Casey," Madison said, pointing at the man, who smiled, exposing rows of teeth so brilliantly white that there was no way they weren't veneers, "This is Antonio—from Verve."

"A pleasure to meet you, ladies," Antonio said, holding out his hand and shaking Casey's and Phoebe's hands in turn. As Casey stared at Antonio, a polite smile plastered all over her face, a tiny spark of hope began to catch fire in her heart. She took in the dark, obviously costly suit Antonio wore and the crisp white dress shirt, his sculpted jawline and the dark hair that flopped down stylishly over his forehead, the dark eyes that watched Madison's every move, and, most of all, the way Madison was looking back at him—like she wanted to eat his suit for a light snack. Casey's happiness ballooned larger still as

Antonio reached down, taking Madison's hand quietly in his own. Casey could barely contain herself, her body flooded with excitement and relief. Could she have been overreacting this whole time? After all, if Madison really *was* dating Antonio, there was no way she could still be interested in Drew—right? And from the way Madison was gazing adoringly up into Antonio's face, it seemed that Casey had her answer. All she needed now was to find Drew . . .

"There you are!" Melanie exclaimed, placing one pale hand on Madison's shoulder. Melanie had the deathly pallor of someone who hadn't seen the sun for eons—basically, a Pulse lackey. Or a vampire. *Same difference*, Casey told herself, trying not to giggle out loud. "We *really* need to get all you girls miked up," she explained, smiling flirtatiously at Antonio. "You'll need to come with me for a few minutes." Casey bit her bottom lip, trying not to smile. It was amazing how the mere presence of a totally gorgeous man could turn a witch like Melanie into an actual polite human being.

Madison rolled her eyes in annoyance, taking a quick glance down at her gown to make sure her prize assets were still in place. "Ugh." She groaned. "I hate those ugly, bulgy battery packs— they make my ass look like the *Titanic*. But, whatever," she laughed, her mood lightening as she gazed up at Antonio. "It's a small price to pay for immortality."

"No part of you could ever look anything less than perfect, *cara*," Antonio said in his devastating, completely melodic Italian accent that made Casey think of water falling smoothly over stones, or some other romantic hooey. He brought Madison's hand up to his lips and kissed it softly while staring into her eyes as if by simply gazing at her, he could somehow crawl inside her body. Phoebe turned to Casey as they began to follow Melanie toward the back of the club.

"Wow," she mouthed, her silver eyeliner glittering under the colorful lights sweeping over the room. Just as they were about to follow Melanie into the ladies' room, Casey saw Drew out of the corner of her eye. He was standing at the bar, craning his neck as he scanned the room, his eyes searching the crowded dance floor. If he'd ever looked cuter, she'd definitely blocked it out. Tonight he was wearing a vintage cream suit with a pink silk tie knotted at his throat. Just looking at him made Casey wish it could be 1976 forever. Who needed twenty-first-century stuff like cell phones and e-mail when your almost-boyfriend looked so totally hot in vintage?

Casey raised a hand above her head, waving frantically to get his attention. As his eyes locked on hers, Casey watched with relief as a huge smile swept over his face, his deep blue eyes lighting up with happiness. But just as she was about to ditch immorality for one night with her maybe-boyfriend, she watched as Drew's gaze moved away from her, his expression darkening. Casey turned around to see Madison whispering into Antonio's ear, her hand resting lightly on his shoulder as his hand circled her waist protectively. As Antonio leaned in, whispering back, Casey couldn't help but notice that Madison's eyes weren't focused on the horse covered in silver glitter wandering around the room, or the faux celebrities who had somehow risen from the dead, but on her ex-boyfriend—the guy she wasn't supposed to care about anymore. As Antonio probably whispered sweet Italian somethings into her seashell ear, Mad's glossy, crimson lips parted slightly, her eyes narrowing in triumph as she took in Drew's jealous gaze. For Casey, time stood still, the room moving in slow motion as she watched the guy she'd been crushing on since she came to Manhattan so obviously pining over his ex. It seemed like hours passed before Melanie appeared back at Madison's side, pulling her into the ladies' room once and for all.

"Well, are you coming?" Melanie said with obvious annoyance, turning around to face Casey, pushing back her tangled red curls speckled with silver glitter with one hand. Casey felt like her Choos were glued to the floor. How could she have been so stupid as to think that straight hair—or anything else—would make any difference at all when it came to getting (and keeping) Drew's attention? *You didn't really think you could compete with her, did you?* her inner bitch said nastily as her eyes smarted with tears.

If dating Drew was a game, Casey was painfully aware that she hadn't had enough practice to understand the rules—and it wasn't like they really mattered anyway, not to girls like Madison who did and got exactly what they wanted by breaking them. As Casey walked into the bathroom, she couldn't help but look hopefully over her shoulder for one final glance at Drew—who had turned back to the bar and was now staring glumly into a bubbling glass of champagne, his almost-girlfriend seemingly all but forgotten.

it's like
thunder . . .
and
lightning

Drew stood at the bar, staring deeply into his glass of champagne, lost in thought. It was bad enough that he had to put on this white, Saturday Night Feveresque monkey suit just to get in the door of Sophie's exclusive Studio 54 redux bash— but did he really have to watch his ex hang all over some totally random guy, too? If Mad wanted to date someone else, that was fine by him. They weren't together anymore and, after all, he wasn't exactly single himself—though the way his supposed girlfriend had run into the bathroom without even coming over to say hi was definitely more than a little weird. Had Casey suddenly become hot-and-cold girl—the type that acted as if she wanted you desperately one day and then couldn't be bothered with your ass the next? If she was Madison, it would be par for the course—but he'd expected a lot more, and better, from Casey.

Drew ran a hand through his tousled dark hair, and stared out at the dance floor where a cowboy dressed in black leather chaps was attempting to climb into the saddle of one of the white horses milling around the club, clearly traumatized by the loud disco beats, and the crush of couture-covered bodies. *That horse is probably on more Valium than Madison's mom,* Drew thought, scanning the crowd for a glimpse of Casey's yellow hair.

God, he was such an unbelievable idiot for not running after her during the interview—and every time he'd seen Casey in the hall the past week, or thought about calling her, he just seemed to freeze, unable to pick up his cell, or walk over and apologize the way he knew, deep down, that he should. But if he actually apologized, then it was true—he really *was* acting a little too into Madison during that interview. Drew sighed, draining his glass of champagne and signaling the bare-chested bartender for another. Oh well, it probably wasn't anything a drink or two couldn't fix. And if that failed, he'd just keep on drinking until he couldn't remember much at all . . . Even if Mad was a free agent, Drew couldn't help feeling a little hurt— the other day during the interview, he'd thought she was definitely flirting with him, and, as much as he didn't want to admit it, he found himself actually kind of *liking* the idea. He didn't *want* to like the idea—even though his pants swore up and down that they were sort of in love with it. But his pants didn't have the greatest track record when it came to dating. In fact, they always seemed to lead him in the wrong direction where girls were concerned.

Drew smiled tentatively as he spied Casey coming out of the ladies' room and heading toward him. She was teetering on a ridiculously steep pair of heels, and rocking a pair of jeans so tight that they made her legs resemble those of a newborn colt. He still couldn't get used to her newly straightened hair—every time he saw her, he found himself doing a double-take. With her hair falling sleekly around her face, her cheeks appeared less round, her face more angular and grown-up looking. Drew raised a hand, beckoning her over, and Casey flushed pinkly and walked over, her eyes focused on the glitter-strewn floor.

"Hey," Drew said, leaning in and kissing her on the cheek. Close up, Drew noticed that Casey had covered up her freckles with makeup, and the sight of her perfectly smooth face made his heart sink a little. Without her freckles and curly hair, she looked almost like a department store mannequin—or every other girl who attended Meadowlark Academy. "You look great," he said, giving her a slow smile.

"So do you," Casey answered back, a little too quickly, then looked down at the floor again. "I like the suit," she said, reaching up and smoothing his lapel with her fingers.

"I waved at you before," Drew said, wrinkling his brow, "didn't you see me?"

"Umm . . . yeah," Casey answered, looking up and meeting his gaze. "I had to go get miked for the show." Casey rolled her eyes and pointed at a battery pack sticking out in a giant lump beneath the tight denim of her jeans.

"Does that mean cameras will be following us around all night?" Drew said with a groan.

"I'm afraid so," Casey grimaced, then smiled for the first time since she'd walked up to him. At the sight of her smile, Drew felt for the first time since the disastrous interview with Mad that everything might just be okay. When Casey smiled it was like the sun coming up—like she was smiling for you and only you. When she looked at him like that, her whole face lighting up like a kid on Christmas morning, it made him feel about ten feet tall, like he could do anything—and faced with that smile, at this moment the Madison Macallisters of the world suddenly didn't seem to matter much at all.

"Think you can handle it?" Casey asked flirtatiously as he reached down and took her hand in his own.

"Guaranteed," Drew answered, closing his fingers around Casey's small hand, and feeling his world, which had been tilting crazily on its axis a moment before, had somehow righted itself. "Let's boogie," he said, pulling her toward the dance floor as the music crashed around them, and some washed-up seventies singer demanded that they better knock on wood. But just as they finished pushing through the crowd and reached the edge of the dance floor, the music faded out and a spotlight steadied on the DJ booth at the far end of the room as Randi Gold appeared, wearing a bright pink leisure suit with a magenta and silver tie knotted at his throat. His hands sparkled with jeweled rings on each finger and a pair of pink-tinted vintage Dior aviators covered his eyes.

"Ladies and gentlemen," his booming, slightly effeminate voice yelled out, "I give you the Queen of the Night, the birthday girl herself, Miss Sophie St. John!" The spotlight panned up to the ceiling, and, instead of the go-go dancer, it was Sophie who sat astride the flying crescent moon as it swung crazily back and forth over the immense crowd. Drew had never really thought Sophie was that pretty—he'd always considered her kind of generic, like every other clone on the Upper East Side—but tonight even he had to admit that she looked stunning. Sophie's gown fell to her ankles in a sheaf of liquid gold, a long slit up the side displaying a flash of pearly thigh. The dress tied halter-style around her neck, and was cut down in the back almost to her butt, exposing a large swath of smooth skin. Her honey-colored hair was styled like Farrah Fawcett circa 1975, in buttery dips and peaks that framed her heart-shaped face and murky green eyes outlined in dark liner, the lids a glittering, shimmering gold.

The crowd erupted in a cheer that seemed to shake the whole club—even over the remix of Donna Summer's "Last Dance" that was now blaring through the speakers. As exciting a moment as it was, Drew was becoming rapidly aware that the three glasses of champagne he had thirstily downed now needed a quick exit from his painfully overfilled bladder. Drew let go of Casey's warm hand, leaning over and yelling into her ear so that she'd hear him over the screams of the crowd and the thumping bass beat.

"I'll be right back," he yelled. "Stay right here so I can find you again." Casey nodded, a smile lighting up her face as she clapped her hands together along with the crowd. If she'd ever looked more beautiful, he'd clearly blocked it out. Impulsively, Drew leaned over and kissed her on the mouth, her lips parting at his touch. When he pulled away, they were both grinning at each other like lunatics before he reluctantly turned around and walked quickly toward the bathrooms, the smile that was plastered over his face a moment ago rapidly disappearing as he caught sight of what looked like his father, standing in a darkened corner near the restrooms, immersed in a heated conversation with a woman Drew could only see from behind—a woman who had clearly disregarded the party's theme by wearing a short, nondescript black dress, her dark, shining hair pulled back in an elaborate twist. His father, on the other hand, fairly screamed seventies bridge-and-tunnel in a white suit that looked like an exact copy of the one John Travolta made famous on the dance floor in *Saturday Night Fever*. Drew watched as if hypnotized, his feet stuck to the sticky, glittery floor as his dad reached out a hand, smoothing a stray lock of hair back from the mystery woman's face, then leaned in, enfolding her in a passionate, lip-locked embrace.

Drew felt like he could barely breathe, the air catching in his chest with a sudden pain that radiated through his torso, then down through his limbs like an out-of-control fire. He blinked hard, trying to clear his vision and make the image of his dad making out with someone who was definitely not his mother disappear completely. But when he opened his eyes again, the same image burned through his brain, and at that particular moment, what Drew felt more than pain, than anger even, was complete and utter shock—mixed with a healthy portion of disbelief. There had to be some kind of explanation. His parents had been madly, crazily, obsessively in love for as long as Drew could remember, and there was no way his dad would just throw it all away for some random, badly dressed and terminally bored Upper East Side housewife, who happened to be impressed by his dad's culinary pedigree. Would he?

Before he could stop himself, Drew walked over behind his father, tapping him on the shoulder. His dad whirled around, his face still wearing a smile that slowly began to evaporate as he regarded his son, his large, burly body shielding the mystery woman's face.

"Hey, Drew," his father said uncertainly, reaching up to rub his salt-and-pepper beard the way he always did when he was nervous, or lost in thought. "Is this some party, or what?"

" 'Or what' is more like it." Once he opened his mouth and began to speak, Drew couldn't keep the anger and disappointment from his voice. It flooded out of him like poison. "So, have you seen Mom around?" Drew asked innocently, "or are you too busy flirting to go look for her?"

"Look, Drew, you don't—"

"Understand?" Drew finished, interrupting his dad's impending speech. "You're right, Dad—I don't. And I'm not sure I want to either." Drew looked over his father's shoulder as the mystery date moved into view, trying her best to hide her face from his view by looking off to the side and raising one pale hand to her heart-shaped face.

"Robert, I'm going to leave you and Drew to—talk things over," she said, looking Drew full in the face for the first time since he'd rolled up on them. Drew stepped back as if he'd been slapped. The anti-seventies woman playing kissy-face with his happily married father was none other than Madeline Reynaud—Phoebe's mom. With that, Madeline turned on one black stiletto heel and walked quickly away, her black dress receding into the sea of pale-hued couture that crowded the dance floor, leaving Drew alone with more questions than he knew his father could probably answer. The fact was that there was no fucking way that any answer his dad could come up with would be good enough to explain why he was cheating on a woman as amazing and beautiful as his mother.

"So, does Mom know about this?" Drew asked, trying to look anywhere but into his father's blue eyes—eyes that pleaded with Drew to listen and understand.

Robert Van Allen ran one hand through his dark hair, and in the mindless gesture, Drew couldn't help but see himself reflected back as clearly as if he were standing in front of a mirror. "It's complicated," his father began, sighing heavily. "Your mother and I have always—"

Drew felt the anger inside him bubbling to the surface, and at his sides his hands curled into tight fists, his knuckles draining of color. "Forget it!" Drew yelled out. Although they'd disagreed more than once over the years, Drew was acutely aware that this was the first time he'd ever dared to yell at his father, and it felt strange—like wearing someone else's shoes that were a size too small. "I mean, how can you possibly justify this? To *me*?"

"Drew, listen." His father reached out, placing a hand on Drew's shoulder. Without even thinking, Drew shrugged off his father's touch, throwing his hands up between them like a shield. "Don't fucking *touch* me—save it for your girlfriend," Drew snarled, turning his back on his father's sad, bewildered face, and walking off into the crowd, the room blurring and turning before his tear-filled eyes. This whole time he had thought he was so different than everyone else at Meadowlark—that he was somehow more special, luckier than all the other divorced-family Upper East Side brats. But now the truth came crashing down on him like a recently demolished building: He was no different than anyone else at Meadowlark or the entire Upper East Side. His idyllic family life was a lie—a complete and utter façade. As he pushed through the crowded room, Drew knew that there was only one person in his life who would understand exactly what he was feeling right now—the one person he knew that he should not, under any circumstances, seek out . . .

But as his father had just made so glaringly clear, Van Allens were aces at doing exactly what they shouldn't.

mommie
dearest

"You look so beautiful tonight, *cara*."

Madison smiled as Antonio whispered in her ear, reaching over and picking up two glasses of pink champagne from the bar, handing one to her. Usually, Madison would've been sulking in a corner somewhere over Sophie's grand entrance that had everyone staring, speechless, as the cameras captured her glittering, glowing figure atop that swinging silver moon. But as she stared into Antonio's dark eyes, to her surprise Madison found that she couldn't have cared less—if Sophie wanted all the attention focused on her, she could have it. After all, it *was* her birthday. The fact was, for the first time in what seemed like forever, Madison didn't care if anyone was paying attention to her—all she wanted was right in front of her.

Madison reached a hand behind her, adjusting the battery

pack that stuck out of her dress like a spinal deformity. Now that Sophie had made her grand entrance, the party was in full swing as waitresses on roller skates expertly circled the room, platters of smoked salmon and caviar toasts balanced on their hands, the dance floor packed with sweaty, slithering bodies moving in time to the music.

"Shall we dance?" Antonio asked, draining his glass of champagne and placing it on the bar, holding out his arm.

"I have a better idea," Madison purred, taking Antonio by the hand. "Why don't we find someplace quiet where we can sit down and . . . talk." Of course, talk, in Madison-speak, meant make out like crazed jackrabbits—but what Antonio didn't know wouldn't hurt him . . . yet. Besides, as much as she really didn't want to, she knew she was going to have to break the news that she'd changed her mind about the whole modeling thing.

"As you wish." Antonio smiled as he clasped her hand more tightly, leading her through the crowded, pulsing dance floor and over to the V.I.P. area, which was furnished in lush red velvet banquettes, the room aglow with hundreds of white tapered candles that shimmered in the soft crimson space.

Madison pulled Antonio toward an empty banquette in a darkened corner, sitting down on the smooth velvet and crossing her legs high up on her thigh—making sure Antonio got a peek at her truly awesome stems.

"So," Antonio said, pulling a pack of Gauloises from the inside pocket of his cream Versace blazer, "what would you like to discuss? I am entirely at your disposal."

"Oh, I don't know," Madison answered flirtatiously, her

green eyes hooded and sleepy-looking. "Why don't we talk about why you haven't kissed me yet—that might make for an interesting topic." Madison leaned closer, reaching out and resting her hand on Antonio's thigh. *God, what am I doing? Get a couple of glasses of champagne into me and I'm a total whore*, she thought with no small degree of amusement.

Antonio lit the tip of his cigarette, blowing a sweet-smelling cloud of smoke over her head, and removed her hand, placing it carefully back in her lap.

"Listen to me, *cara*. I am your manager—we work together. That means any relationship I have with you must be strictly business."

"Blah blah blah," Mad said with a wave of her hand. "Save the speech for some Ukrainian fishstick just off the boat, okay, Antonio? I know all *about* the modeling industry—I saw *Gia* on HBO."

Antonio laughed softly, flicking cigarette ash into the darkness. "I am serious," he continued, turning back to face her.

Madison looked at his chiseled face, how the candlelight illuminated his dark eyes. "Then I just won't be your client—I told you—I'm not sure I really want to model anyway." Madison moved her lips into the seductive, slow smile that usually got her whatever she wanted, and looked up expectantly at Antonio, whose face seemed to harden before her very eyes.

"Then why are you wasting my time, *cara*?" Antonio snapped, a look of annoyance spreading over his sharp features.

Madison drew back from his sharp tone, leaning her body farther away on the red velvet banquette. Her face flushed red with embarrassment and outrage. Who did this Euro-hottie think he was anyway? *No one* talked to Madison Macallister that way—she didn't care how many Cindy Crawfords or Naomi Campbells he'd discovered!

"I didn't think I was wasting your time, Antonio," Madison answered between gritted teeth. "I thought we were . . . getting to know each other."

Antonio looked silently off into the distance, his gaze following the screaming partygoers as Sophie appeared on the dance floor, a white spotlight illuminating her dress and hair as she threw her arms confidently overhead, posing for the Pulse cameras and the pack of photographers that Phyllis had undoubtedly hired for the event.

As she surveyed the commotion, Madison gave a quick sigh of relief. Although she was definitely miked, thank God a photographer hadn't had the foresight to follow her and Antonio to the V.I.P. room. It was bad enough that she felt completely humiliated by Antonio's brush-off, but at least it wasn't on camera . . . Madison shifted uncomfortably in her seat, wondering if she should just walk away from this entire mess. Obviously she'd read the signals wrong, and, as unbelievable as it seemed, he just wasn't interested. *What's wrong with me?* Madison lamented silently. *First Drew, and now this.* But, maybe she was just being silly and letting the whole thing get to her too much—after all, even if Antonio was an older guy, he was still just a guy. Period. And if anyone at Meadowlark had ever dared speak to her the way Antonio had, she would've left them eating a cloud of her dust as she briskly walked away—*after* she'd had the last word, of course. Then why was she so confused about what to do now? *Well,* she thought, running a hand through her hair while trying to think of something to say to break the awful tension that had come down like an iron curtain between them, *at least the night can't get any worse . . .*

"Madison, darling! *There* you are!" Madison looked up in disbelief as Edie made her way across the V.I.P. room, heading straight for them.

"Oh my God," Madison murmured, her mouth falling open as Edie approached. *You have got to be kidding me . . .* Edie stood in front of them, smiling brightly, her long, lean body clad in a vintage white silk Halston jumpsuit that tied around the neck with a series of gold chains, and plunged low in front, exposing far more of her mother's tanned skin than Madison wanted to see at any given time. A pile of hammered gold bangles adorned one of Edie's arms, and her Chopard diamond teardrop earrings sparkled against her golden bob.

"Who is this *divine* man you're sitting with?" Edie said flirtatiously, batting her long eyelashes in an ultra-feminine performance that made Madison want to vomit all over her mother's gold Christian Louboutin stilettos.

"His name is Antonio—from Verve Model Management," Madison snapped as Edie sat down on the banquette beside her, forcing Madison to move over to make room.

"So lovely to finally meet you, Mrs. Macallister," Antonio purred, reaching over Madison's body to grasp Edie's hand, shaking it softly as Edie blushed and giggled like a twelve-year-old schoolgirl. *What the fuck?* Madison fumed silently. *Am I even still here?*

"It's *Ms.*," Edie replied, still holding on to Antonio's hand. "And, please—call me Edie."

Madison rolled her eyes, convinced that if she had to witness one more moment of this disgusting spectacle Edie was making of herself, she'd lose what was left of her mind—not to mention her dinner. Madison stood up, smoothing down her dress with one hand as she pushed past Edie, giving her mother an extra shove as she squeezed past her knees.

"Are you leaving already, dear?" Edie inquired, her eyes still locked on Antonio.

"Are you kidding?" Madison said, the last bits of Sex Kitten Madison quickly falling away, her voice rough and raw. "I should never have been here in the first place," bitchy Madison spat. "Have a lovely fucking evening," she added as she turned away, one hand violently wiping at a single renegade tear that somehow had managed to escape her well-controlled ducts.

Smoothing her dress and adjusting that damn mike-box-thing so it didn't shatter any vertebrae, Madison walked in slow, measured paces through the V.I.P. area, willing her emotions to disappear before she crossed the velvet ropes and stepped onto the dance floor. She forced herself to imagine gigantic cups of Pinkberry, champagne at Dior in Paris, her shoe collection, anything to eradicate the sticky nastiness that being shot down by Antonio had brought to the surface. Not to mention the fact that he was clearly more interested in her overmedicated old witch of a mother than her. *Italians*, Mad thought to herself, *I should've known better. They'd crawl right back into the womb if it was allowed.*

Just as she was feeling a false sense of well being that she was depending on to make it through the night, just steps away from the crowded anonymity of the dance floor, Mad caught the writhing movements of some makeout session out of the corner of her eye. *This could be a good bit of gossip*, she thought to herself, peering into the velvet shadows to see Phoebe locked in the arms of . . . Oh my God! Madison clasped one hand over her mouth as if she had actually spoken aloud—and even if she had it wasn't like anyone was going to hear her over the truly awful seventies music that was ringing in her ears.

Phoebe was standing in a darkened corner holding hands with Sophie's ridiculously hot, but totally annoying brother, Jared, her face tear-streaked and pained. Madison still hadn't forgiven Jared for putting ice in her bed during a sleepover at Sophie's when they were eleven. What the hell was going on with everyone tonight? Had all of her friends lost their minds en masse? First Sophie had miraculously become some sort of disco-goddess/TV star, and now Phoebe was canoodling with Sophie's *brother?* How long had this been going on? Not very long, Madison suspected as she watched Jared reach up and wipe a tear from Phoebe's gleaming cheek. Madison had known Sophie long enough to know instinctively that there wasn't a chance in hell that Sophie would be even remotely happy about these damp and sticky developments—Sophie practically hated her brother! Since Jared had been kicked out of his ultra-posh boarding school he'd become the bane of his sister's existence—and with good reason. Mad had always thought Jared's surfer bullshit was completely annoying in every way possible. And he really wasn't that cute either—he just *thought* he was, which, in boy-language, often got confused with being one and the same.

Madison forced herself to tear her eyes away before Phoebe looked up and noticed her standing there, and walked determinedly to the bar and downed a glass of champagne. It was definitely time for a drink. It was much better to simply pretend that she'd seen nothing than to confront Phoebe. One thing Madison knew from experience was that there was nothing finer than information—and information was power. As she stood there, still in shock, Drew raced by in his vintage suit, looking as adorable as ever.

"Drew," she yelled out as he passed, reaching out to grab the cream-colored sleeve of his jacket. At the sound of her voice, Drew stopped his frantic movement, smiling weakly before looking over his shoulder as if someone was chasing him.

"Hey," he said, his voice sounding strange and strained, "I'm on my way out—but I really need to talk to you later."

Oh . . . really? Madison smiled slowly, her eyes narrowing. It was amazing—and so very predictable. Madison just knew that the minute Drew saw her with another guy he'd come running right back to her where she belonged. Well, at least she'd gotten something out of the whole Antonio fiasco. . . .

"Why?" Madison asked coolly. "What could we *possibly* have to talk about?"

"More than you think," Drew shot back, his face a mass of worried wrinkles. His blue eyes looked bloodshot and damp, as if he'd been crying. The longer he stood there looking so confused and upset, the more Madison was almost starting to feel bad for him . . . *almost.* But not quite. *Whatever—he probably had some stupid fight with Little Miss Perfect,* Madison thought as she stood there weighing her options. *Boo-hoo for them.*

"I'll call you later," Drew said in a rush, the sweat gleaming on his brow as he look over his shoulder one last time, and headed off into the crowd, the crush of bodies swallowing his white suit until he disappeared completely from her sharp, green-eyed gaze.

"Of course you will," Madison whispered with a triumphant smile, always happy to have the last word—even if no one else was around to hear it.

change
partners

Casey stood a few feet away from the dance floor, rest-ing her back against a white pillar, trying to look as though she was having a good time. Every few minutes she'd crane her neck, looking around the crowded room for Drew. When that failed, she tried searching for anyone that she knew at all—but Phoebe had disappeared as soon as they were all miked up, Madison was "occupied" with Antonio, and Sophie was flitting around the room saying hello to three hundred of her closest friends and playing hostess. That left . . . nobody.

Drew had been gone for close to a half-hour, and as the minutes ticked by and time dragged on, Casey found herself wondering if he was ever coming back at all. Casey sighed, rais-ing her glass of champagne to her lips and taking the tiniest of sips to make it last longer. Just when she thought things were going to be okay with her and Drew, something like this happened, and she found herself questioning everything all over again. Dating was totally exhausting. She'd almost rather be at home right now, curled up in bed watching funny videos on YouTube or practicing the new Vivaldi piece she was trying to learn on her own . . .

Just as she was about to give up, she saw Drew pushing through the crowd, his face tight and angry, his cheeks reddened. Whatever had kept him away for so long clearly wasn't good. He looked like he was ready to pick a fight and punch someone out, just for existing. Casey smiled as he approached, her heart pleading with her brain to convince her that everything would be all right, while her brain, realist that it was, knew better.

"I was getting worried," Casey said jokingly, trying to keep her tone light, as if she didn't mind being left alone for the past million years. "I was afraid you'd been kidnapped by Andy Warhol and the rest of The Factory and forced to do vile things with aluminum foil and Brillo boxes."

Drew let out a laugh that came out like a cross between a bark and a cough, and looked down at the floor, agitated and clearly not amused by her attempt at seventies, avant-garde humor.

"Listen, Casey," Drew began, and, as Casey heard the words come out of his mouth, her heart began to dip in her chest. She knew all too well—even from her limited experience with guys—that when a sentence began with "listen," the news usually bordered on disastrous. "I've got to go. I'll see you around, okay?" Drew's eyes nervously searched the perimeter of the room, settling anywhere but on Casey's face.

"But . . . you just got here," Casey said, totally confused by Drew's complete one-eighty.

"I know," Drew said, shoving his hands in his pants' pockets and avoiding her eyes.

Casey frowned, trying not to get screamingly annoyed and freak out all over him. What was she supposed to do? Yell? Tell him not to leave? Both? Unfortunately, neither option felt exactly right. If something was really wrong, why didn't he want to talk to her about it? Or maybe he was too embarrassed to ask. After all, guys were definitely weird about any kind of emotional messiness.

"Do you . . ." Casey began, cringing slightly as the words left her lips, "want me to come with you or anything?"

"No thanks," Drew answered in a voice so tight and clipped that she stepped back in shock, colliding with the Grace Jones clone who glowered at her from behind a pair of black sunglasses. "Listen," Drew mumbled, "I've really got to get out of here. I'll see you later." He pushed past her without another word or an explanation, and headed for the front door of the club before she had time to think of anything else to say or do.

Casey stood there feeling completely dejected and dangerously close to tears before realizing that a camera operator standing a few feet away was pointing his lens right at her face. Casey looked straight into the lens, giving the cameraman a small smirk while simultaneously raising and extending the middle finger of her right hand—and then promptly turning around.

It was bad enough that Drew—who was obviously not going to be her boyfriend any time soon—had just walked out on her in front of practically the entire school and most of the Upper East Side, but there was no way she was going to give Pulse's entire drama-hungry TV audience the pleasure of seeing her cry on top of it. She'd already been humiliated once at Drew's welcome home party a month ago, and once a year was enough for anyone—even Casey McCloy.

"Excuse me," a timid voice interrupted. Casey turned around and practically knocked over undead Warhol, who was regarding her with a cool, disinterested expression underneath his shockingly white, messy wig. "Have you seen Edie? I've been looking for her simply *everywhere*," he went on in a voice so breathy it suggested that he'd been doing laps around the dance floor instead of quietly surveying the crowded room.

"No," Casey answered, fighting back the urge to burst out laughing. "I haven't."

"Oooooooooooooo—I adore your top—gold thread is so *sparkly*!" he cooed, nodding approvingly in the general direction of Casey's shirt, although he was so spaced out it was hard to know what he was nodding at for sure. "Did you see the birthday girl?" he asked conspiratorially, leaning closer so that Casey could see the thick, white pancake makeup that was layered on top of his pale skin like Spackle. "Gee, what a beauty!" Before Casey could think up a witty response, Warhol shuffled off slowly—presumably to retire to his coffin for the evening.

"What was *that* all about?" a voice on the other side of the pillar she was leaning against asked in a tone that suggested that they, too, were about three seconds from totally losing it. A scarily thin guy with a shock of black hair that fell across his forehead over one dark eye, wearing a vintage black Sex Pistols T-shirt and a white blazer with a pair of dark APC jeans stared back at her, his red lips curling into a smile. *Why did he look so familiar?* Casey wondered as he held out one bony hand for her to shake, his tight grip belying his frail demeanor. She was sure she'd seen him before somewhere . . . but where? Ugh. Casey wrinkled her nose, totally disgusted with herself. She hated when this kind of stuff happened to her—she was terrible with faces and even worse with remembering names. Whenever a situation like this arose, it almost always meant she was about to feel like an idiot. *I'm sure tonight will be no exception*, she thought with dismay as he let go of her hand, shoving his hands into the pockets of his blazer.

"I'm Darin Hollingsworth," he said, giving her that look—the one that basically screamed, "Why don't you recognize me?" When that failed to ring any bells, Darin continued. "I slapped you on the back a few weeks ago in the hallway? You were choking or maybe having some kind of bizarre epileptic fit?"

Relief broke out over Casey's face, and she smiled widely in recognition and relief. It was the Emo guy who had clapped her on the back outside of French class. She hadn't thought about him one way or the other when it had happened, but now, looking at him standing there, she realized that he was . . . not bad looking at all. Actually, he was more than that—he was really sort of cute in a worshipping Conor Oberst, dyeing all his clothes black, and living in Williamsburg kind of way . . . Before she could process her own thoughts, alarm bells went off in

Casey's head, and she began to feel monumentally guilty. Was she even allowed to think another guy was cute when she was kind of involved with Drew? Except, she wasn't kind of involved with Drew anymore—was she? And didn't Nanna tell her that the best way to make a guy jealous was to play the field and give Drew a taste of his own medicine? *Besides,* she told herself, *I'm not doing anything. There's no reason I can't talk to the guy. It's not like Drew has stopped talking to other girls just because we were kind of a thing. Unfortunately.*

"So, are you loving this, or what?" he asked with a smirk that brought out an adorable dimple in his lower left cheek.

"It's everything I dreamed it would be," Casey said laughingly, relieved to be talking to someone who was obviously on her wavelength.

"I promised myself that I wouldn't go to another one of these things this year—and yet here I am," Darin said, holding his arms out helplessly. "Wearing a vintage blazer and waiting for someone to wheel out a cake. How do you explain this?"

"You're probably a masochist," Casey said with a giggle. "I don't know how else to explain it."

"You're so right," Darin said with a faux tortured sigh and a half-smile. "I hate sweet sixteen parties—and yet, I'm inexplicably drawn to them. It's a conundrum, wrapped in an enigma—wrapped in bacon . . ."

Casey laughed out loud, throwing her head back. God, it felt good to talk to someone who saw this whole Meadowlark scene for what it was—totally phony. All at once she was a little disgusted with herself for trying so hard to fit in when it was probably a losing battle anyway. She wasn't exactly to the manner born like Phoebe, Sophie, or Madison, and it was reassuring to know that there was someone else out there like Darin—who didn't care about fitting in, and who seemed just fine with being a little different from every other Meadowlark robot draped in Prada and Gabbana.

"So, I know this music is pretty lame and everything," Darin said with a grin, "but I think it would be pretty cool to get out there and show these future trustfund zombies how it's done. You game?"

"Absolutely," Casey said, taking Darin's hand and following him out to the floor. As the colored lights streamed across their bodies and the music throbbed all around, reverberating off of the walls of the club, Casey felt her heart lift with happiness as all the messiness and unresolved things between her and Drew faded away into the background as Darin smiled down at her, pulling her close and bending her back into a deep dip that made her hair brush the silver, glittering floor.

And across the room, the Pulse cameras zoomed in, capturing every second on film before they cut to Madison's lone figure, still standing at the bar, her eyes locked on the spectacle of Darin and Casey, a canary-eating smile creeping across her parted lips.

baby
i'm a
star

Sophie straightened her ivory fedora and turned around in the expansive space of the private dressing room, checking her gleaming white suit. The dress she'd worn for her grand entrance was gorgeous—but she could hardly dance in it. The dressing room was usually reserved for acts like Britney Spears or Puff Daddy to chill in before they took the stage, and as a result, practically every wall was shimmering with mirrors. The room was designed for constant, relentless narcissism, but seeing herself reflected so many times in a relatively small space kind of freaked Sophie out. Could anyone really be that into themselves that they'd want to look at their body from every possible angle? It was a question she wasn't sure that she really wanted an answer to . . .

Sophie took a deep breath, staring into the nearest wall of

mirrors to calm her admittedly jangled nerves. So far the party was more than a total home run—it would definitely be remembered as the party of the year. But all Sophie could think about was her bio mom and why she hadn't shown up yet. And as the night got progressively later and later, Sophie started to wonder whether or not Melissa would even bother to make an appearance at all. Maybe she didn't really want to see her. After all, Sophie told herself, she could've just said she'd come to be polite. *She doesn't owe you anything,* Sophie whispered into the mirror, her eyes filling with tears. But *didn't* she? Didn't she owe her *something*—even if it was just an appearance at her sixteenth birthday party?

Her cell phone began to beep noisily, breaking her thoughts as she pulled her iPhone from her ivory Balenciaga motorcycle bag and pressed TALK.

"Sophie, honey, I think you'd better come down now," her mom said, her voice sounding strained, like she'd been crying. "Randi's going to bring out the cake soon, and . . . there's someone here who wants to see you."

Sophie's heart skipped a beat, and then stopped dead in her chest.

"She's here?" Sophie whispered. "She's really here?"

"Just come down, hon," Phyllis answered, obviously refusing to offer any more information. "I love—"

Sophie pressed END before Phyllis could finish, feeling like she was in a daze. "This is it," Sophie whispered to herself, taking one last look into the mirror before walking out into the club. The next time she looked in the mirror, she wouldn't be the same hopeful Sophie who was looking back at her now.

She might be better off or she might be heartbroken, but all Sophie did know for certain at that moment was that whatever happened when she went downstairs and walked up to her mother for the first time, she'd definitely be *different*. This moment was going to change everything, and, if she went through with it, nothing would ever be the same again.

As she descended the stairs, Sophie felt like she was vibrating—it was the same kind of feeling she'd get sometimes when she'd had too many lattes. She couldn't seem to stop shaking. She wasn't scared exactly, or nervous, but the tension of not knowing what to expect was definitely starting to get to her. *Maybe Casey and Mad were right,* Sophie thought, her green eyes anxiously scanning the crowded room. *Maybe this is putting too much pressure on just one night . . .*

"Sophie!" a voice called out as she reached the bottom of the stairway. Sophie watched as Phyllis parted the crowd and moved toward her, a tight smile on her lips. As she approached, Sophie felt her breath catch in her throat as she realized that the woman trailing behind her mother—accompanied by a mass of cameras and lights—was none other than Melissa Von Norton, her real mom. Phyllis stopped right in front of her, the sounds of the crowd and the reporters clamoring for Melissa's attention buzzed like a pesky mosquito in Sophie's ear. Phyllis grabbed onto Sophie's arms, staring up at her with red-rimmed brown eyes, obviously in the kind of pain Sophie could neither soothe or forgive. But Sophie's heart couldn't help but soften as she looked at the woman who had raised her all these years, who had always gone out of her way to provide Sophie anything she could ever ask for—even if it was done out of guilt rather than love—and she almost wanted to ask everyone to go home right then and there, to call the whole thing off so that her life could go back to the way it was, when she thought things were normal. And then—as if in slow motion—Melissa moved from behind Phyllis and stood in front of Sophie like a mirage, a soft smile curving the corners of her full, exquisite lips. She stared at Sophie in wonderment, reaching out one hand to touch a lock of Sophie's hair that echoed the same golden color as her own honey-hued locks. Melissa grinned her hundred-watt movie star smile, her teeth shining brilliantly against her pale, peaches-and-cream complexion as she reached up, tweaking Sophie's fedora with an index finger. *She has the same hands as me*, Sophie thought incredulously, unable to take her eyes off of them. *The exact same hands.*

"Happy birthday, kiddo," Melissa said, her voice low and gravelly. Sophie was speechless. All she could do was stare at her mother, her eyes greedily taking in the impeccably cut white wool pants she wore, and the black silk shirt, the gold and pearl Chanel necklaces looped endlessly around her long, pale neck, the pearl crosses and gold double-C charms hitting her abdomen. Her face was even more striking in person that it was on film—perfectly oval with deep-set murky green eyes the exact shape and color of Sophie's own. Her hair hung to her shoulders in loose, honey-colored waves, and her skin was as pale as milk. *It's like looking into a mirror*, Sophie thought, paralyzed.

"You're here," Sophie said quietly, aware that the Pulse cameras had moved in for the kill and were recording her every move. To make matters more complicated, paparazzi had infiltrated the club and were circling the pair like vultures. Flashbulbs exploded in Sophie's face and she blinked rapidly, momentarily blinded by the powerful lights that made her dizzy. "You're really *here*."

"Of *course* I'm here!" Melissa said jovially, reaching over and placing her arm around Sophie's shell-shocked shoulders, leading her out of the crowd. "I told you'd I'd come, didn't I? I've wanted to meet you for a long time now, Sophie. You can't imagine how long." Melissa turned to face her, her expression grave as she touched Sophie's cheek with her fingers, tears swimming in her green eyes, her touch cool and light on Sophie's skin. As she stared into her mother's eyes, she felt a void inside her begin to close. *It's like a dream.* Sophie thought as she reached up, taking her mother's hand in her own as the cameras went ballistic, the reporters smelling a good story as they moved in, sticking tape recorders and microphones into Melissa's face and shattering the moment between them.

"Melissa, why didn't you ever admit to having a daughter? When did you get pregnant? What made you decide to get in contact with Sophie?"

The reporters' questions filled the air and Melissa threw up her hands, her expression playful.

"Whoa! Hang on a minute!" She yelled good-naturedly, throwing her head back as she laughed, and in the one, insignificant gesture, Sophie saw herself. Watching her mother and seeing her own tics and mannerisms in this woman she didn't know, who she'd never met before, was downright spooky. "One question at a time, okay?"

A blond, female reporter stepped up, rudely shoving a microphone under Melissa's aquiline nose. "Melissa, when is *Speed Quest* going to be released? Is it true that you and costar Jude Law have become more than just friends?"

"You'll have to check with the studio about the release date," Melissa said, turning her attention to the camera that was busily filming her every word. "They've pushed it back so many times now that I've lost count. And Jude and I are dear friends," Melissa said with a wink and a smile into the lens. "*Very* dear friends."

At that, the reporters went wild, pushing in closer and closer until Sophie found herself shoved into the background, the crowd threatening to swallow her whole on its celebrity-obsessed wave. Sophie watched with rapidly growing disappointment as her mother patiently answered question after question, smiling happily into the camera—and not once turning to look in Sophie's direction. *Is this all I get?* Sophie thought incredulously, her hands balling into fists at her sides. As she watched her mother ignore her, use her for a goddamn photo op, Sophie felt herself growing smaller and smaller, shrinking into the background as the crowd clamored around Melissa—her party, the fact that Melissa Von Norton was her mother, her entire presence clearly forgotten. There was an ache in Sophie's throat, and a turning in her stomach as she silently pleaded with Melissa to turn around and remember that she was standing there, to tell her that it had all been an oversight, that she'd been overwhelmed by the crowd, the cameras, the flashing lights—by her own emotions. At that moment Sophie would've believed any explanation, as long as there *was* one.

All her hopes came crashing down as Melissa allowed herself

to be led to the V.I.P. room, walking away without a backward glance and leaving Sophie standing near the dance floor as practically everyone she knew stared at her piteously, taking in the scene with whispers hidden behind palms and sly glances. Gathering all the dignity she could muster, Sophie turned her back on the scene sharply as the DJ began blasting Calvin Harris's "Acceptable in the 80s," and the room filled with the hyper-happy sounds of crashing synth beats. Sophie began walking blindly toward the back of the club, her vision blurred by her unspilled tears, her glitter-dusted cheeks flushing hotly. *If I can just make it to the bathroom,* she thought silently, feeling as though she were underwater as she pushed through the flailing arms and legs of the crowd, the shrieking laughter of delighted partygoers ringing unpleasantly in her ears. *If I can just get out of here for a minute, I'll be all right.*

Just as she was about to push through the bathroom door, lock herself in a stall, and contemplate never coming out again, a rustling movement and a flash of silver glitter hidden in the shadows caught her eye. Sophie peered through the darkness and walked a little closer as she realized that the flash was Phoebe's shimmering silver dress. Sophie breathed a sigh of relief, ecstatic to have found someone she could pour her heart out to. But as she got closer, she realized that Phoebe was definitely not alone—Phoebe was pressing up against a shadowy figure dressed in black, her lips moving rapidly in what seemed to be a heated conversation. Well, whatever was going on, it could definitely wait—she was in the middle of a crisis! Phoebe could go back to getting her flirt on after she'd properly consoled her.

"Hey!" Sophie called out as she approached. "God, am I

glad to see you, Pheebs. Everything's a complete disaster, my mother—"

Phoebe look at Sophie, wordless, a sheepish and slightly terrified expression moving over her heart-shaped face, her dark eyes darting from Sophie to the shadowy figure standing against the wall. Sophie could see that Phoebe's bright, magenta lip gloss—which had been perfectly applied at the start of the evening—was now hopelessly smudged in one corner. She'd clearly been getting up close and personal with whoever was lurking in the shadows. Sophie squinted her eyes and moved closer to the shadowy lump half-hidden behind Phoebe, the shock registering in her eyes as she came face-to-face with a figure that was scarily, horrifyingly familiar.

"Jared?" Sophie demanded as her pulse quickened, her blood boiling like lava in her veins. "What's going on?" Sophie turned to Phoebe, feeling like everything familiar and safe had just been ripped away from her in the last twenty minutes. First her own parents betrayed her—and now her brother, too? *At least we're keeping it all in the family*, Sophie thought bitterly. This was like some bad acid trip. Could someone have spiked her champagne or something? Try as she might, there seemed to be no other explanation for the total randomness that she was now experiencing. "*Phoebe?*" Sophie stared at her best friend, her gaze murderous.

"Sophs," Phoebe said quickly, regaining some of her composure, "it's not what it looks like." Sophie narrowed her eyes, crossing her arms over her chest. "I mean it *is* . . . but it's not like we wanted to lie to you, it's just—"

"No, that's fine, really," Sophie said, cutting Phoebe off

before she could get another word in, her voice like ice. "Haven't you heard? *Everyone* lies to me. Why should you be any different? But I guess that's the problem, isn't it?" Sophie went on, a tear escaping her right eye and sliding down her cheek before she could stop it. "That I thought you were different. I thought you were my *friend*."

"Sophs, listen." Phoebe's face crumpled along with her composure, and she extended her hands, trying to grab onto Sophie's arm, her eyes pleading, her expression mirroring the one Sophie had seen and subsequently ignored in Phyllis's eyes earlier that evening. And as Phoebe's hands reached out, Sophie backed up rapidly, smacking into a disco cowboy wearing a pair of metallic gold leather chaps.

"Don't *touch* me!" Sophie yelled putting out her own arms in front of her to ward Phoebe off. "Don't talk to me. Just leave me alone."

"Listen, sis, you need to chillax," Jared said as calmly as if he'd been languidly waxing his surfboard for the last ten minutes. He threw his head back, shaking the hair from eyes covered by chrome aviators, and straightened the bottom of his ridiculously retro beige Members Only jacket. "Let's just go and sit down and we'll—"

"Don't you *dare* talk to me right now," Sophie screamed, tears streaming down her face, streaking her gold shadow and liner. "And that's not even seventies!" she yelled, pointing at his jacket. "It's *eighties*!"

Before either of them could say another word Sophie spun on her heel, almost toppling over completely before she righted herself and tore off into the crowd. *Just get me the hell out of here*, she prayed silently as her eyes darted from side to side, looking frantically for the exit. As she pushed through the gyrating crowd on the dance floor, a familiar voice came over the sound system. Sophie turned and looked up at the DJ booth. Melissa Von Norton stood there, a microphone in her hand, beaming down at the crowd.

"Can I have your attention, please? I've brought a very special gift for the birthday girl—my dear daughter, Sophie!" The crowd gasped, turning around en masse to face Sophie, who stood there as motionless as a wax figure. "Will everyone be so good as to follow me outside?" Melissa said with a twinkle in her eye as the crowd rushed toward the front door of the club like someone had announced that Zac Efron was standing directly outside, on the pavement in front of Marquee, completely naked. *That would give a whole new meaning to curbside service,* Sophie thought as she moved numbly through the crowd, ignoring the constant chatter that surrounded her, feeling as totally and completely alone as she ever had in her entire life.

Instead of a naked teen sex symbol, a brand-new black BMW convertible was parked at the curb, a bright pink ribbon wound around the hood ending in a garish, glittery bow. As Sophie stood staring at the car like it was a dinosaur that had somehow crawled its way back to the island of Manhattan, Melissa came up behind her, resting one peach-manicured hand lightly on Sophie's shoulder, and pressing the shining silver car keys into Sophie's palm with the other.

Sophie stared down at the keys in her hand, resisting the urge to gouge them into the soft flesh of her arm, the roar of the crowd seemingly miles away as she looked up uncomprehendingly into her mother's face. This time—though the resemblance was clearly still there—she saw none of herself reflected back in her mother's placid, empty green eyes. "I don't drive," Sophie said woodenly, shoving the keys back into her mother's hand, and shrugging off her touch with a brisk shake of her shoulders. "But you wouldn't know that about me, would you? Because you've never been *around*."

"Sophie, I . . ." her mother began with a worried smile, looking nervously at the flocks of photographers that had gathered around them like birds.

"You *what*?" Sophie snarled, letting the anger and disappointment she felt wash over her in what felt like an emotional tidal wave. "You came here to use me as a photo op—that's what." Sophie's eyes darted around the circumference of the crowd and rested on Madison standing there. *Stop*, she mouthed, rolling her eyes for added emphasis. But Sophie felt like she'd gone too far already, that stopping, or even slowing down was completely out of the question, not to mention impossible.

"Sophie, that's not true," Melissa said firmly, reaching out and grabbing onto Sophie's arm. "I came here for you."

"You came here for *this*!" Sophie yelled, pulling away from Melissa's grasp as if her mother's touch burned through the fine silk of her jacket. She pointed an index finger accusingly at the rapidly popping flashbulbs, the crowd pushing in for a better look, her murky green eyes red and wet. "And you can have it."

Sophie turned and ran, her legs moving as fast and as hard as she could. She ran like someone was chasing her, like her life

depended on it, turning down the city streets, her heels clicking against the still-damp pavement from the rain shower that
had sprinkled Manhattan a few hours earlier, her arms moving
in time with her breathing as her nose began to run and the
fedora flew off her head, twirling once in a gust of wind, then
smacking against the windshield of a yellow cab with a barely
audible thud.

one big
happy
family

"Drew, wait!"

Drew ignored his father's voice, picked up the pace, and kept walking, his hands shoved into his pockets, his head down to hide the tears that had sneaked out from the corners of his eyes. When he didn't slow down or answer, his father began to run, and Drew heard a rush of footsteps on the pavement as his dad fell into step alongside him, breathing heavily.

"Listen," his father said breathlessly, stopping in the middle of the sidewalk to crouch deeply, bending over at the waist, his white jacket pulling tightly over his slightly rounded stomach. Robert Van Allen was still carrying around one too many pounds from his days working as a chef—too many slivers of foie gras and spoonfuls of cream-based sauces had somehow found their way around his middle over the fifteen years he'd worked in the kitchen. *The guy couldn't even run half a block and he was having an affair?* Drew thought, looking at his father with undisguised disdain.

"Drew," his father said, once he'd regained his breath, his face red and sweating, "we really need to talk."

Ten minutes later, Drew found himself regarding his father stonily from his perch on a cracked and peeling leather barstool at O'Malley's, a faux Irish pub a few blocks from Marquee. The air was hazy with smoke, and his dad raised his hand in the air, signaling for a refill of the Glenlivet on the rocks he'd just downed in a few easy swallows. Drew scuffed the toe of his vintage Converse high-tops against the sawdust-covered floor, angling his body as far away from his father as he could possibly get without getting up and moving to another seat.

"Are you sure you don't want anything to eat?" Drew's father asked, looking over at his son, his brow lined with worry.

Drew shook his head and looked away—determined not to look back. "Water's fine," he said, his voice tight, his hand circling the rim of his glass. Drew still couldn't believe what he'd just seen back at the club. He had the happiest parents in all of Manhattan, didn't he? Whatever his dad had to say couldn't *possibly* explain why he'd been having an affair with Phoebe's mom, of all people. He'd never had even one nice thing to say about Madeline Reynaud. Drew had heard his dad complain that Madeline was a bourgeois, stuck-up snob more times than he could count—and now he was *dating* her?

And adding insult to injury was the mind-boggling fact that Drew's mother, Allegra Van Allen, happened to be an internationally acclaimed, award-winning artist. Not only was she talented, she was also witty, intelligent, and still unbelievably beautiful. What more could his father possibly want in a woman? *How could he not love her anymore?* Drew wondered, his mood darkening even more than he thought possible. Their seemingly happy relationship was now a total and complete mystery to him. As he sat there silently contemplating his rapidly melting ice cubes, Drew couldn't stop himself from wondering the obvious: Had they been faking it all these years?

"Do you love her?" Drew blurted out, taking a sip of his ice water, hoping the cold liquid would cool him off enough so that he could be rational.

"Who—Madeline?" Drew's father chuckled as if the question were totally preposterous, picking up his full glass from the bar and knocking it back in one swallow. "Of *course* not."

"Then, *why?*" Drew asked, now more confused than ever. Why would his father risk everything—his home, his family—for some woman he didn't even love? It didn't make any sense.

"Listen, Drew. Of course I love your mother—of course I do." Robert Van Allen turned to his son, putting his empty glass on the bar with a sharp click. "But we have an . . . arrangement."

"What *kind* of arrangement?" Drew turned to look at his father, needing at last to see his face. His dad was always the person Drew went to when he had a problem, the one person Drew trusted implicitly—and he was a liar. As complicated as his dad wanted it to be, the truth was that it was plain and simple. His father had lied to him all these years.

"Your mother does as she wants—and I do the same. Usually discreetly and *without* the intrusion of TV cameras," his father said with a grimace.

"So, Mom . . ." Drew's voice trailed off into nothingness. The sounds of the pinball machine in the back of the bar suddenly seemed very loud, the smoke hanging in the air chokingly thick.

"True intimacy," his dad began, stroking his salt-and-pepper beard thoughtfully, his blue eyes focused on Drew's face, "is letting another person see you completely—faults and all. I'm not perfect, Drew—far from it—and I've never been able to be completely faithful to any woman. But your mother accepts me anyway—and we've made it work all these years."

"That's what you call making it work?" Drew said slowly, unable to keep the disgust from his voice. "Sorry, but I don't see it," Drew said, pushing his melted ice away and folding his arms over his chest—more for protection than anything else. Drew felt like he was going to shatter into a million sharp pieces if his father said even one more word.

"You'll see what I mean someday, Drew," his father said knowingly as the bartender refilled his drink. "You're just like me, you know."

Drew flinched at his father's words, the anger that he'd tried to stuff back inside him rising to the surface and spilling out before he could put it in check. "I'm nothing like you, Dad." Drew stood up and faced his father head-on. "*Nothing.*"

Robert stood up from the table, reaching out for Drew's shoulder, trying to comfort him, trying to calm him down. Drew's own arm snapped out, on its own accord, knocking that instinctual fatherly gesture aside as if it had been a shove, a punch. Drew felt as if his head were in the oven at one of his father's restaurants, a lump of meat being broiled with a flash of incendiary heat. His pulse thudded behind his eyes and he stepped forward, not knowing if he should run, scream, punch his dad in the face, or if he should sit back down in the booth and never stand up again. Robert's eyes looked soft, worried, when he looked into them—trustworthy eyes, the eyes of his dad. Robert reached out again and grabbed onto Drew's shoulder, pulling him forward.

"I'm sorry," he said, "you shouldn't have seen that, shouldn't have found out this way."

Those words, the unbelievable reality of the cheating father they referred to, stood in such sharp contrast to the feeling of those familiar arms around Drew's shoulders. It was so tempting to believe those arms, to believe that what he saw, what he now knew, changed nothing. But the last thing Drew wanted right then was for his father to be right. He was nothing like him. *Nothing*, he repeated to himself, breaking away from his father's embrace. He stepped back and looked up to see his father's face wet with tears. He turned his back and walked toward the door.

Nothing.

But somewhere deep inside a voice rose up inside him, a voice so quiet Drew could almost pretend he hadn't heard it at all. More than anything, Drew wanted to shove that little voice back inside him, hold it down, and suffocate it with a pillow. That smug, irritating, inquisitive little voice that wondered if maybe, just maybe, his father was right after all.

there's got to be a morning after . . .

Madison awoke amidst the snowy perfection of her white Porthault sheets and Siberian goose-down pillows plumped like whipped cream beneath her head, her green eyes opening slowly as she surveyed the clean, modern perfection that was her room. She placed her hands behind her head, the events of the evening flooding back into her brain. *God, what an unbelievable fustercluck*, she thought, shaking her head from side to side on her pile of pillows as she remembered Sophie's tear-streaked face as she ran down the block and out of sight.

The night had gotten worse from there on. Antonio completely disappeared at some point in the evening—presumably with Edie in tow, which made Madison feel like she might just barf up the seventy-two or so glasses of champagne she'd managed to pour down her throat last night all over the snow-white rug covering her bedroom floor. That Antonio could possibly prefer decrepit Edie to her was not only unbelievable, it was also kind of nauseating—which wasn't exactly helping her hangover . . .

As she was contemplating whether to order some fruit and a bagel from Mangia, or stick with black coffee and Tylenol, her bedroom door swung open, and Edie entered the room clad in a midnight blue silk La Perla robe, her crimson pedicure shining like rubies against the white carpet.

"Rise and shine!" Edie trilled, walking over to the row of large windows behind Madison's bed and flinging the heavy, white silk drapes open, flooding the room with sunlight. Madison growled unintelligibly, shoving her head under the pillow.

"I hate you," she said crankily, as her mother plucked at the pillows covering Madison's matted blond hair, pitching them softly to the floor.

"I'll pretend I didn't hear that," Edie said cheerily. *A little too cheerily*, Madison thought suspiciously as her mother sat down on the edge of the bed, crossing her smoothly waxed legs. Edie was always a total nightmare in the A.M. If she was in this good of a mood before she'd even taken her morning Valium, then something *must've* happened last night to make her very happy indeed. *I really* am *going to throw up*, Madison groaned silently as she curled on her side, trying to get as far away from Edie as possible without actually getting out of bed.

"I had a long talk with Antonio last night." Edie dreamily ran a hand through her silky blond bob—even at the crack of dawn, her mother's hair was predictably perfect. It was completely infuriating, kind of like Edie herself. "And I want you to know that I've thought long and hard about it, but you're a Macallister—there's no way I'm going to let you parade yourself down a *runway*." Edie's blue eyes widened as she reached out, patting Madison's leg beneath her comforter. "I don't want you to end up like some common hotel heiress with a sex tape before you're twenty-two, and your own *revolting* perfume they won't even sell at Saks!"

"Whatever." Madison moaned, pulling the comforter up around her shoulders and wishing Edie would just disappear. "I don't *want* to model anyway."

"Well, thank God for that!" Edie said with relief, standing up and pulling the tie of her robe more tightly around her minuscule waist. "Now I have to get back to bed." Edie giggled, covering her mouth with one hand like a schoolgirl. "I'm not exactly alone—if you know what I mean!"

Madison sat up in bed and glared at her mother, wishing she had a bow and arrow she could shoot at her—or a gun. Wasn't it bad enough that Edie stole Antonio from right underneath her nose? Did she have to bring him home and rub the whole thing in her face, too? "Get out of here!" Mad yelled, picking up a pillow from the floor and lobbing it across the room where it struck Edie squarely in the face.

"Was that really necessary?" Edie replied in a voice so syrupy that Madison almost wanted to drag her mother down to Serendipity and throw ice cream on top of her. "Some people have no manners," Edie continued, kicking the hurled pillow out of her way as she opened the door, stepping out into the hallway. "No manners at all . . ."

Madison flopped back down on the bed, closing her eyes and wishing she'd never woken up. The day had just started and already it was a total suckfest. She found herself wondering what else could go wrong when she actually made it out of The Bram. Maybe I should just stay right here today, Madison thought as she rolled herself up in her sheets like a tamale.

Just as she was sliding back into sleep, her phone erupted in a series of beeps and chirps that made her want to hurl it out the window unanswered. She opened her eyes and reached down to the floor to retrieve it, glaring at the tiny screen. Unidentified caller? Even though it was probably a telemarketer or some other annoying bullshit, she pressed TALK anyway—she really needed someone to yell at this morning, and telemarketers were easy targets.

"Helllllllllo?" she said, mid-yawn, clapping a hand over her mouth.

"Is this Madison?" a perky female voice inquired.

"In the flesh," Mad said crankily, kicking the covers from her bare legs and sitting up. "Who's this?"

"This is Melanie, from Pulse—we've met a few times over the last couple of weeks?"

"Uh-huh," Madison grumbled, already bored with the conversation. She had less than nothing to say to some redheaded troll who was clearly in need of a date—not to mention a makeover of epic proportions.

"We were watching the footage from Sophie's party last night," Melanie continued, "and your . . . performance really jumped out at us. We'd like to talk to you about the possibility of creating a reality series based on your life . . . and your friends',"

Melanie said in a rush. "Is there any way you could come down to our office on Monday—say around three?"

Madison's mouth fell open as she contemplated what she'd just heard. Her mind raced as the future this call could make possible played itself out in high-def—the free clothes, the red carpet, the promotional events in Paris, Tokyo, fucking Sumatra. She'd be presenting awards to her biggest pop-star crushes at the Pulse Video Music Awards before she finished high school. And then a crossover to the big screen . . . a fashion line . . . a *fabulous* perfume that wouldn't even sell at major department stores like Barneys or Saks because it was *too good.*

She caught her breath and willed herself to stay calm, to keep her voice—which wanted to start screeching her impending divadom from the top of the Chrysler building—at an even keel. "Monday," she said into the phone, her voice ringing with feigned uncertainty, "I *guess* I could do Monday. I'll have to move a few things around, you know, but I should be able to make it."

"Wonderful," Melanie exclaimed, her voice immediately filling in the slow, calculated coolness of Madison's words. And Madison suddenly found that perky voice to be anything but annoying—her mind was talking to her at just the same pitch, speed, and candor. She was completely, unbearably excited. "So we'll see you Monday at three?"

"I'll see you then," said Madison, pulling the phone away from her ear, her finger hovering around the END button.

"Oh, and Madison," she heard Melanie's voice, tiny and small, float up to her from the phone, held at arm's length. She moved it back to her ear. "Could you bring Casey along with you? I've been trying and *trying* to get a hold of her, but I just can't seem to get in touch. You see, the producers want to do something with *both* of you . . . wouldn't that be exciting?"

Madison quickly rewound the highlight reel of her soon-to-be-future, quickly Photoshopping Casey into each frame: Casey walking with her down the red carpet, flashbulbs popping as they stopped to glare at one another under the assault of white lights; Casey with the new Marc Jacobs calfskin bag that she wanted slung carelessly over one arm; Casey handing a gold trophy to Justin Timberlake, and air-kissing each stubbly cheek; Casey being as famous, as loved, as *cool* as Madison Macallister. The bright white of her room suddenly went gray as a cloud passed between her windows and the sun, a shiver running over her body. "I'll let her know," she said into the phone, through tightly clenched teeth.

"Thanks, dear. You must just be so excited. The two of you are going to be *amazing*. We'll see you on Monday."

On Monday indeed.

And now a special excerpt from the next book
in the Elite series . . .

SIMPLY IRRESISTIBLE

Coming from Berkley JAM
July 2009!!!

plaza suite

Madison Macallister tossed her platinum blond hair back from her shoulders and snuggled more deeply into the cable-knit, ivory cashmere sweater that hung to her thighs. Her legs, encased in Habitual dark washed skinny jeans that were so tight they appeared painted on, looked even longer and more stem-like than usual due to the stretchy denim that hugged every morsel of flesh from her nonexistent waist to her delicate ankles. *Skinny jeans are better than a fucking corset,* Mad thought as she leaned ever so slightly across the table and reached for the gleaming white-and-gold porcelain teapot. Not that she needed one—with her statuesque figure, glowing skin, green, slightly upturned eyes, and endless legs sheathed in winter white, knee-high suede Marc Jacobs boots, Madison Macallister was an icon of Upper East Side teen perfection—and she intended to keep it that way. And now that there were cameras in her face on a daily basis, obsessively roaming over and recording every inch of her envied and celebrated body, she couldn't afford to be careless about what she shoved in her mouth . . .

Madison poured the fragrant Lapsang Souchong tea into a thin, Spode teacup and raised it to her cranberry-glossed lips—courtesy of YSL—ignoring the tall silver tray of tiny cucumber sandwiches and perfectly plump petit fours iced in sugary shades of lavender and rose, and looked around at The Plaza Hotel's freshly revamped dining room, sighing happily. When she was a little girl, she'd read the *Eloise* books over and over until their pages were stained and tattered, entranced by the antics of the precocious six-year-old who ran the lavish Upper East Side hotel as if it were her own private three-ring circus. After all, one of Madison's most beloved games as a child was pretending she *was* Eloise and that her stuffed monkey, Binky (who'd been loved so hard that his fur was missing in clumps), was Eloise's Nanny. Madison would sit on the floor of her bedroom, a Fisher-Price telephone in her lap, and make pretend calls to room service, ordering—in a voice that was already slightly imperious—a cup of tea for Nanny and two sunflower seeds for her turtle Skipperdee, "and charge it please. Thank you very much." Ever since Madison was old enough to read, Edie would take her to The Plaza every December for a "girls' day out," which usually included a long afternoon tea with plenty of sandwiches and cake, and then a mani-pedi at Elizabeth Arden where Edie would proceed to pop Valium like a maniac, then babble nonsensically to Madison, the manicurist, the empty chair across the room—until Madison finally peeled Edie's Amex from her wallet and handed it over to the receptionist—who'd most definitely seen it all before, many times over.

Even though The Plaza had been freshened up a bit, Madison was relieved to see that nothing had really changed—there were still the same opulent, enticingly fragrant bouquets of flowers on every available surface, still the same garden-themed dining room with its airy, muted fabrics, still the same oil portrait of Eloise that hung just off of the lobby, her small, mischievous face framed in softly glowing gold leaf. And December was the perfect time for a visit since the hotel was draped every holiday season, without fail, in sparkling-white fairy lights and sweet-smelling pine garlands. A huge Christmas tree sat in the center of the dining room, snow-colored lights twinkling merrily, red velvet bows and gleaming silver balls affixed to its towering branches. Coming to The Plaza with Edie for their holiday ritual was the only time Madison actually looked forward to spending time with her annoying and pharmaceutically obsessed mother all year long—until now.

Ever since Pulse had begun filming *De-Luxe*, a new reality show that was being touted as "a look inside the lives of the Upper East Side's REAL Gossip Girls," she'd barely had a moment to herself. Each day was filled with school, and then shoots that often stretched on well into the evening. Even now, the bright halogen lights shone in her face, making her sweat in a way she hoped wasn't too obvious on camera. Mad bit her bottom lip and prayed that the droplets of sweat that were threatening to make their way out of her pores wouldn't begin slowly rolling down her face. She wrinkled her brow as she re-membered last week's shoot on the front steps of Meadowlark, how they had been forced to pause constantly so the makeup artist could blot Casey's disgustingly sweaty face. *At least I only sweat when there's some obnoxious, nuclear-powered light in my face*, Mad thought, running the tip of her tongue surrepti-tiously over her teeth to be sure they were lipgloss-free. Casey was such a total disaster in every way possible that it was hard *not* to look good next to her on camera.

But if Mad had learned anything from seeing herself on tape, it was that the camera, with its sweeping, meticulous gaze, no-ticed absolutely everything. Not to mention the fact that *De-Luxe* had no script to speak of—not that it was a problem. If there was one thing that Mad knew she excelled at, it was in-venting drama—and Madison Macallister practically had a PhD in creating her own real-life soap opera. But she had always as-sumed, much like everyone else in the world, that the reality shows on Pulse were completely scripted, so she'd been sur-prised when the producer, Melanie, had been so hands-off with their dialogue from the very beginning,

"Why the hell would we script it?" Melanie had barked the day Madison and Casey arrived at the Pulse offices to sign their contracts. Melanie pushed her tangle of red curls away from her pale face with exasperation before continuing, slamming her hand down on the table for emphasis. "Your real life is *bet-ter* than any crap we could make up!"

"Tell me something I *don't* know," Madison snapped, reach-ing over and grabbing the pen from Casey's hand and scrawling her signature at the bottom of the stack of pages piled in front of them.

Needless to say, the late nights and the grueling schedule were really screwing with both her social life *and* her academic performance, which, as of late, had been less than stellar— not that she was all that worried about it. Madison's problems, academic or otherwise, usually had a way of working themselves out—in her favor, of course. . . . There was also the added headache of having to see the insufferable Ms. McCloy both in and out of school on a goddamn daily basis. Actually, she wasn't really *that* bad. . . . Madison shook her head rapidly, trying to wipe the thought from her brain. God, all this holiday cheer and ho-ho-hoing was really getting to her. Well, at least she hadn't said it out loud. . . .

Madison watched as her mother, Edith Spencer Macallister, brought her teacup to her lips, her expert maquillage and freshly blown-out blond shoulder-length mane obscured by a cloud of sweet-smelling white steam. Edie had taken to the cameras like a debutante to couture, and, as a result, her face looked tighter and even more plasticky than usual—thanks to the increasing visits to her dermatologist's office. Now that she and Antonio were officially an item, Edie, paranoid and random as ever, had decided that she needed all the help she could get in order to "keep up" with not only the TV cameras, but her younger man as well. To make matters worse, Edie had just embarked on some ridiculous detox diet where the only thing that would pass her seriously augmented lips for the next two weeks would be bottles of pee-colored lemon water mixed with cayenne pepper and maple syrup. The thought of it was enough to make Madison almost regurgitate her Lapsang Souchong over the spotless white tablecloth.

Actually, she didn't know what was more nauseating—Edie's diet, or the fact that Edie and Antonio, a gorgeous, Italian scout from Verve Model Management who had stopped Madison on the street in October, were now an item. Even though she'd decided pretty quickly that the life of a supermodel wasn't for her, what made the whole thing even harder to take was that she hadn't exactly felt the same way about Antonio. The night of Sophie's sweet sixteen, he'd ended up going home with her mother, of all people. The thought was enough to make her gag reflex stop working permanently from bouts of constant dry heaving.

"Darling," Edie beamed, placing her cup back onto its saucer. "I don't want to ruin our time together today. But we do need to talk about something rather *serious*." Edie's smile was replaced by a worried look as the camera moved in for a close-up. *Crap,* Mad thought, exhaling loudly and looking down at her tea. *Here we go . . .* "I've spoken to your academic advisor at Meadowlark and your recent grades are completely unacceptable."

Edie's voice was suddenly as brittle as the icicles hanging from the tops of the buildings lining Fifth Avenue—and every bit as cold. The gold Kenneth Jay Lane bracelets lining her wrists jingled with a tinny, metallic sound as she waved her hands expansively for emphasis. "If you're going to have even the *faintest* shot at getting into Harvard, you are going to have to step things up. And if you don't," Edie paused to dig in her beige Chanel tote for an amber-colored prescription bottle, swallowing a small, yellow pill before continuing, "then I'll be forced to pull you from the show—no exceptions. You need to concentrate on your *future* for a change."

Madison rolled her eyes and picked up a small pink cookie, biting down angrily. *Screw calories.* As the shiny icing broke between her teeth like crusted snow, Mad knew that as much as it killed her to admit it, for once her mother was actually right— she had been ignoring her schoolwork—along with most everything else in her cluttered, jumbled, seriously over-committed life. But it was kind of hard to concentrate on the pointlessness of world history or algebra when total stardom was waiting just around the corner . . .

"Edie, *cara.* There you are." Madison whipped her head around at the sound of Antonio's mellifluous Italian accent, her cheeks bulging with un-chewed pastry. Mad swallowed hard, brushing the crumbs from her jeans. This was clearly just what she needed—it was bad enough that her own mother had stolen her almost-maybe-potential-boyfriend right from under her nose, but did Madison really have to sit here and watch these two over-the-hill lovebirds moon all over each other in broad *daylight?*

"Antonio!" Edie trilled, holding out her cheek for Antonio to kiss as he slid into the chair beside her. "So glad you could make it."

"Bella," Antonio said softly, looking over at Madison, his dark eyes the color of the ultra-decadent chocolate truffles at La Maison du Chocolat. "So good to see you again."

Even with a massive case of five o'clock shadow obscuring

his chiseled jaw and wearing a rumpled, navy velvet blazer, Antonio was still annoyingly hot. Mad rolled her eyes and looked away as Antonio took Edie's hand in his own, kissing it lightly.

"Oh my *God*," Mad said as Antonio pulled himself away from Edie's overly manicured paw. "Am I hallucinating? Edie, what is *he* doing here?"

"Well, I just thought that he could—" Madison cut Edie off by putting her palm in the air and raising one eyebrow in disbelief.

"Antonio?" Madison trilled sweetly. "Have you suddenly grown a vagina? Because we're supposed to be having a *girls'* day out."

Madison's sweet smile turned into a satisfied smirk as she watched Antonio's smile fade and his face become suffused with color as he looked quickly away from her gaze and over at Edie helplessly. *Don't count on it,* Madison mused smugly as she watched Edie reach for Antonio's hand again, grasping it firmly in her own, her heavily outlined eyes widening in disbelief.

"Just ignore her," Edie said smoothly to Antonio, smiling widely as if a million-watt bulb had just been switched on in her brain. "Madison gets positively *insufferable* around the holidays."

"It's not the holidays, *Mom*," Madison snapped, pulling her phone from her Cesare Paciotti black calfskin bag and checking for missed calls—if only to distract herself from the overwhelming sense of annoyance and anger that was making her blood boil like a steaming jacuzzi. "It's the fact that you thought it was *appropriate* to invite Ricky Martin here to the one family tradition we have *left*."

"Look, *cara*," Antonio turned back to Madison and stared at her, his expression as neutral as Switzerland. "I do not mean to cause any problems between you both, and I certainly do not wish to be where I'm clearly unwanted." Antonio stood up, pulling a pair of black Gucci aviators over his eyes.

"At least he can take a hint," Madison muttered under her breath as she drained the rest of her tea, making a face as it was now ice-cold. As Antonio turned around to leave, Edie jumped from her seat and grabbed onto his arm. Madison's mouth fell open as she watched Edie hanging on Antonio's arm like a three-year-old in a bakery begging for more bon bons. *Desperate much?* Mad thought disgustedly as she rolled her green eyes and popped another heavily frosted petit four into her mouth. God, it was bad enough that Antonio was about a million years younger than her cradle-robbing mother, but did she have to make such an embarrassing spectacle of herself in public? Not to mention on *camera?*

"Antonio, darling," Edie said, reaching up and twining her arms around his neck, "You simply *must* stay for a while. I won't take no for an answer!" Madison watched in horror as Antonio smiled down at Edie then bent his lips to hers, brushing them lightly. When their lips broke apart, they stood there gazing into each other's eyes like they were hypnotized. *Am I still here?* Mad thought in disbelief, her mouth falling open as she watched Edie lead Antonio back to the table and sit down next to him, reaching for the silver tray and popping a hunk of cake into his mouth while they cooed nonsensically at each other like a pair of demented, designer-clad lovebirds.

Madison crossed her arms over her C-cups and concentrated

on staring at the brightly decorated Christmas tree instead of the slobbering make-out zombies in front of her. How much crap was she going to have to take before the humiliating fiasco that was her mother's love life blew up in Edie's face again? Ever since the divorce, her mother's "relationships"—if you could even call them that—seemed to end as quickly as they'd begun—often with tears and empty bottles of Cristal strewn all over the lavish baroque splendor of the Macallister's penthouse apartment. Christmas, which had always been Madison's favorite holiday, was definitely canceled this year. Without her father it just seemed pointless. She hoped against hope that he might agree to stop by on Christmas day—just for a few hours. But any expectations she had were ripped away like discarded wrapping paper after his secretary informed her that "Mr. Macallister is planning a sailing trip to the South of France over the holidays, and won't be back until the New Year." *Probably with some nineteen-year-old* Penthouse *pet,* Madison fumed, brushing crumbs from her lap. Besides, even if she *were* bursting with Christmas cheer, what would she and Edie do anyway? Bake cookies and sing carols? Not likely. *Screw the Christmas spirit,* Madison glowered as Antonio looked over, shooting a weak smile in her direction.

"Your mother has invited me to spend the holidays with you both—and I have accepted," Antonio said carefully, wiping the crumbs from his full lips with a white linen napkin.

"Great. I'll alert the media," Madison snapped as she stood up, throwing her black cashmere military-inspired D&G coat over her shoulders, the silver buttons flashing in the light. "It'll be a miracle if you two survive past New Year's," Mad said as she pulled her arms through the sleeves, not bothering to fasten the buttons and exhaling loudly in annoyance. Not that Edie and Antonio were paying attention anyway—the minute she got up, Edie began whispering in Antonio's ear and giggling like a love-struck teenager. As she looked at them, Madison couldn't help but feel a giant wave of sadness crashing over her—a wave she hoped to God the cameras wouldn't pick up on as she left their sorry asses sitting in cake crumbs.

"Oh, and by the way," Madison said in a tone just saccharin enough to make Edie and Antonio quit their pawing and look up blankly into Madison's sweetly smiling face—if she'd learned anything from Edie over the years it was definitely how to fake it—even when you felt like killing someone. *Especially* when you felt like killing someone. "Bah fucking humbug," she snarled, turning on one heel and marching across the glittering, ornate lobby. *After all*, she told herself, blinking back an ocean of frustrated tears from her eyes, *no one ever could accuse Madison Macallister of being a girl who didn't know how to make an exit . . .*

But even so, as she walked out of the place that represented the happiest days of her childhood and into the frigid air blowing down Fifth Avenue, Madison couldn't help wishing that she had something that even remotely approximated a real family. After all, it was one thing to lose your boyfriend to the new girl in town, but it was something else entirely when guys started dumping you for your mom! Madison bit her bottom lip as she pushed through the front doors, checking her reflection in the shiny glass. Had she lost her trademark Macallister hotness? Was that even possible? Still, why would any guy in his right mind prefer Edie to her? There were cameras trailing her every move on a daily basis, and in a few short weeks the show would premiere and she'd be famous—or infamous. So then why was she suddenly feeling so . . . invisible? Ugh, there was nothing like a breakup to make you feel completely insignificant—no matter who you were. She needed a Breakover—and fast. Madison stepped onto the street, pulling her phone from her bag, her finger scrolling through her call-list, searching for Frederic Fekkai when it erupted in her hands and began buzzing shrilly.

"What?" Madison barked, walking into the street and throwing out one hand to try to hail a cab, her platinum hair whipping around her head in a sudden gust of wind.

"Hey," Drew said nervously. "Glad I caught you."

"I'm in a hurry." Mad rolled her eyes and uttered a sound that closely resembled the piercing, slightly guttural cry of an elephant being shot with a spear. "I'm trying to hail a fucking cab. But what's up?"

"I just wanted to see if we could meet up tomorrow night." Drew cleared his throat, and in the depths of that scratchy noise she could hear how down he sounded. Come to think of it, he'd been weirdly depressed and totally un-Drew-like since Sophie's party—not that it was her problem anymore. "I really need to talk to someone."

"You need to talk to someone," Mad repeated tonelessly as a cab screeched to a stop right in front of her. She grabbed the door handle and fell into the backseat, breathing hard. "God, I fucking hate cabs." The driver shot her a dirty look in the rearview mirror. "No offense," Madison said, holding the phone away from her ear. "Fifty-sixth and Park," she barked at the driver. "Look, Drew, do you need to talk to 'someone' or do you need to talk to me—there is a difference, you know."

God, she sounded like such a bitch sometimes. But she couldn't seem to help herself—especially where Drew was concerned. Ever since last spring when they had sort-of almost lost their virginity to one another, things had definitely been far from perfect between them. Not only had he immediately run off to spend the summer in Amsterdam without even saying goodbye, but he'd started flirting with the bane of her existence that was Casey McCloy—new girl and complete loser—the minute he'd stepped foot back on the island of Manhattan.

"I know," Drew said, exhaling loudly in frustration. "And I need to talk to *you*, okay?"

"Meet me tomorrow night at Space. Nine o'clock."

"*Space?*" Drew said with no small amount of disbelief. "You mean you're actually going to venture *below* Times Square of your own free will?" Drew scoffed playfully, referring to Madison's disdain of anything not Upper East Side, as well as the fact that Space, one of the hottest new clubs in town, was located in SoHo—as far downtown as one could possibly get without being in Chinatown—or Brooklyn. "Who are you?" he demanded jokingly, "And what have you done with Madison Macallister?"

"I'm not even hearing you," Madison said sweetly, staring out the window at the traffic blurring by. "Besides, if it's good enough for the cast of *Gossip Girl*, it's definitely good enough for me."

Drew chuckled, sounding more like his old self than he had in weeks. "All right—I don't usually make it a practice to descend into the inner apex of Hipdom on a school night, but I guess for you I can make an exception."

"Glad to hear it," Mad answered with a hint of her trademark sarcasm, hoping Drew could *feel* how hard she was rolling her eyes at him. After all, he *did* mention once that he thought they had some kind of telepathic connection . . .

Madison pushed END with one French-manicured nail before Drew could say anything else, tossing her phone back into her bag, taking a strand of hair between two fingers and studying it carefully. She was definitely still pissed at Drew—that wasn't even up for discussion—but, even so, she couldn't ignore the fact that meeting him at the hottest new club in the city was the *perfect* excuse to unveil the new, improved Madison Macallister . . .

about the author

Jennifer Banash attended high school on the Upper East Side of Manhattan and currently resides in Los Angeles, California, where she lives with her beagle, Sigmund, and her vast designer shoe collection. She is the author of the novel *Hollywoodland: An American Fairy Tale*, and is the co-founder and co-publisher of Impetus Press, an independent publishing house that champions serious literary fiction with a pop edge. E-mail Jennifer at theeliteseries@gmail.com, or check the latest updates on The Elite series on MySpace at MySpace.com/theeliteseries, theelitebooks.com, or follow Mad, Drew, and Casey on Twitter.com!

Printed in the United States
by Baker & Taylor Publisher Services